ONE NIGHT STANDS

This Limited Edition of
One Night Stands
by Lawrence Block
is one of 450 copies sewn in cloth
and signed and numbered by the author.

Accompanying each copy
is a separately printed pamphlet,
Make a Prison
by Lawrence Block.

Number 289

Lawrence Block (signature)

ONE NIGHT STANDS

Lawrence Block

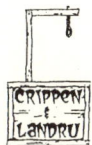

Crippen & Landru Publishers
Norfolk, Virginia
1999

Copyright © 1999 by Lawrence Block

Dust jacket painting and design by Deborah Miller

Crippen & Landru logo by Eric D. Greene

ISBN: 1-8859941-30-7

FIRST EDITION

Crippen & Landru Publishers
P. O. Box 9315
Norfolk, VA 23505
USA

Email: CrippenL@Pilot.Infi.Net
Web: http://www.crippenlandru.com

CONTENTS

Introduction: If Memory Serves 7
The Bad Night 15
The Badger Game 25
Bargain in Blood 36
Bride of Violence 44
The Burning Fury 56
The Dope 64
A Fire at Night 69
Frozen Stiff 73
Hate Goes Courting 81
I Don't Fool Around 89
Just Window Shopping 96
Lie Back and Enjoy It 101
Look Death in the Eye 106
Man with a Passion 113
Murder Is My Business 121
One Night of Death 127
Package Deal 132
Professional Killer 139
Pseudo Identity 148
Ride a White Horse 160
A Shroud for the Damned 173
Sweet Little Racket 182
The Way to Power 190
You Can't Lose 198
Sources 206

IF MEMORY SERVES . . .

In 1956, from the beginning of August through the end of October, I lived in Greenwich Village and worked in the mail room at Pines Publications. I was a student at Antioch College, in Yellow Springs, Ohio, which sounds like a hell of a commute, but that's not how it worked. At Antioch students spent two terms a year studying on campus and two terms working at jobs the school arranged for them, presumably designed to give them hands-on experience in their intended vocational area. Like a majority of students, I had spent my entire freshman year on campus. Now, at the onset of my second year, I was ready to begin my first co-op job. I knew I wanted to be a writer, so I went through the school's list and picked a job at a publishing house.

Pines published a paperback line, Popular Library, a batch of comic books, and a couple dozen magazines, including some of the last remaining pulps in existence. (*Ranch Romances*, I recall, was one of them. It was what the title would lead you to believe.) I worked five days a week from nine to five, shunting interoffice mail from one desk to another, and doing whatever else they told me to do. My weekly salary was forty bucks, and every Friday I got a pay envelope with $34 in it.

I lived in the Village, at 54 Barrow Street, where I shared a one-bedroom apartment with two other Antioch co-ops. My share of the monthly rent was $30, so I guess it fit the traditional guideline of a week's pay. I know I never had any money, but I never missed any meals, either, and God knows it was an exciting place to be and an exciting time to be there. (I was eighteen, and on my own, so I suppose any place would have been exciting, but at the time I thought the Village was the best place in the world. Now, all these years later, I haven't changed my mind about that.)

ONE NIGHT STANDS

I didn't do much writing during those months. I'd realized three years earlier that writing was what I wanted to do, and every now and then I actually wrote something. Poems, mostly, and story fragments. I sent things to magazines and they sent them back. At Antioch, I taped the rejection slips on the wall over my desk, like the heads of animals I'd slain. Sort of.

One weekend afternoon, I sat down at the kitchen table on Barrow Street and wrote "You Can't Lose." It was pretty much the way it appears here, but it didn't end. It just sort of trailed off. I showed it to a couple of friends. I probably showed it to a girlfriend, in the hope that it would get me laid, and it probably didn't work. Then I forgot about it, and the end of October I went back to campus.

Where at some point I remembered the story and dug it out and sent it to a magazine called *Manhunt*. All I knew about *Manhunt* was that most of the stories in Evan Hunter's collection *The Jungle Kids* had first appeared in its pages. I'd admired those stories, and it struck me that a magazine that would publish them might like my story. So I sent it off, and it stayed there for a while, and then back it came.

With a note enclosed from the editor. He liked it, but pointed out that it didn't have an ending, and that it rather needed one. If I could come up with a twist ending, a snapper ending, he'd like to see it again. So I found a newsstand that carried *Manhunt*, bought a copy, read it, and wrote a new ending, one which at least proved I'd read O. Henry's "The Man at the Top." (My narrator ends with the triumphant boast that his ill-gotten gains are due to increase dramatically, because he's just invested the whole thing in some goldmine stock. Or something.)

I sent this off, and it came back with another note, saying the new ending was predictable and didn't really work, but thanks for trying. And that was that.

Then several months later the school year was coming to a close, and I was due to head off to Cape Cod and find a co-op job on my own. One night near the end of term I couldn't sleep, and I lay there thinking, and thought of the right way to finish the story. I went

IF MEMORY SERVES . . .

home to Buffalo to visit my folks, drove out to Cape Cod, and wrote a new ending for the story. The acceptance process was slow—*Manhunt* had what we've since learned to call a cash-flow problem—but, long story short, they bought it. Paid a hundred bucks for it.

My first sale.

I left the Cape after a month or so and wound up back in New York, where I got a job as an editor at a literary agency, reading scripts and writing letters to wannabe writers, telling them how talented they were and how this particular story didn't work, but by all means send us another story and another reading fee.

I lived in a residential hotel on West 103rd Street, where my $65-a-month rent was again a fourth of my salary. And, nights and weekends, I wrote stories, which the agency I worked for submitted to various magazines. Most of the stories were crime fiction. I hadn't yet decided I was going to be a crime fiction writer—I don't know that that's a decision I ever made—but in the meantime I read extensively in the field. There was a shop on Eighth Avenue off Times Square where they sold back copies of *Manhunt* and other digest-sized magazines (*Trapped, Guilty, Off-Beat, Keyhole, Murder,* and so on) at two for a quarter. I bought every one of these I could find, and I read them cover to cover. Some I liked and some I didn't, but somewhere along the way I must have internalized the sense of what made a story, and I wrote some of my own.

They sold, most of them, sooner or later. Sometimes to *Manhunt*, but more often to its imitators. *Trapped* and *Guilty* paid a cent and a half per word, so they were the first choice after *Manhunt* passed. Then came Pontiac Publications, at a penny a word. (Their magazines had titles like *Sure Fire* and *Twisted* and *Off-Beat*, and every story title had an exclamation mark at the end. I longed to call a story "One Dull Night" so that they could call it "One Dull Night!")

After I'd been a month or so at the literary agency, it was clear to me I was learning more than I'd ever learn in college, and that I'd be crazy to stop now. So I dropped out and stayed right where I was. In

ONE NIGHT STANDS

the spring, I decided I'd learned as much as I was going to at the job, and that a student draft deferment was, after all, better than a poke in the eye with a sharp bayonet. I went back to Antioch.

By the time I got there, I was writing books. "Sex novels" was what we called them, though they'd now get labeled "soft-core porn." I wrote one to order the summer before I returned to Antioch, and the publisher wanted more. So that's what I did instead of classwork. And I also went on writing crime stories. At the end of that academic year, in the summer of 1959, I dropped out again, and this time it took. I started writing a book a month for one sex novel publisher, and other books for other publishers, and from that point the crime short stories were few and far between.

When Doug Greene and I discussed bringing out a collection of these early stories, he brought up the subject of an introduction. "You can read through the stories," he said, "and write some sort of preface."

"One or the other," I said. "You decide which."

I have a lot of trouble looking at my early work. I rarely like the way it's written, and I especially dislike the glimpse it gives me of the unutterably callow youth who produced it. I like that kid and wish him well, but read what he wrote? The hell with that.

You know what? I'm *afraid* to read them. I'm scared I'll decide not to publish them after all, and it's too late for that.

So an uncharacteristic attack of honesty compels me to advise you that I am in the curious position of introducing you to a couple of dozen short stories which I myself haven't read in forty years.

Someone else suggested that some of the stories might require revision, because attitudes expressed in them are out-of-date and politically incorrect. No way, I told him. First of all, one of the few interesting things about them is that they're of their time. I'd much rather burn them than update them. And screw political rectitude, anyway. You want to go through *Huckleberry Finn* and change the name of Huck's companion to African-American Jim? Be my fucking guest, but leave me out of it.

IF MEMORY SERVES . . .

A few things you might want to know:

1. A few of these stories, as indicated in the bibliographical notes at the back, were published under pen names. This only happened when I wound up with more than one story in the same issue of a magazine. W. W. Scott, who edited *Trapped* and *Guilty*, would make up a pen name when this occurred, generally by working a variation on the author's usual byline. Thus "B. L. Lawrence." The guy at Pontiac asked what pen name to use in similar circumstances, and I provided the name "Sheldon Lord." Were there other pen names? Maybe, because there have been editors in the business who had house names which they used at such times. Maybe they used them on stories of mine. I don't think this ever happened, but at this point I'd have know way of knowing. And no reason whatever to care . . .

2. There's a story in here called "Look Death in the Eye" that deserves comment. It may strike some readers as curiously familiar. I wrote it way back when, while I was working for the literary agent, and it sold to Pontiac, and I lost all track of it. Didn't have a copy, didn't know where to find one.

And I found myself thinking about the story. What I really liked about it was the last line, and that, really, was all I remembered. So I recreated the story from memory, right up to the last line, which I recalled word for imperishable word. I hammered it out and sent it off to a fellow named Bruce Fitzgerald, who was editing a magazine called *For Women Only*. (It was a beefcake magazine, as it happens, composed of outtake photos from *Blueboy*, a gay magazine. The stories and articles interspersed among the nude male pix in *For Women Only* were ostensibly slanted to female readers, of which I doubt the magazine had more than twenty nationwide. The idea was that, by being purportedly for women, it could get on newsstands closed to gay publications, where its true audience would, uh, sniff it out. Its name notwithstanding, it was really for *men* only. Publishing is a wonderful business.)

ONE NIGHT STANDS

Bruce liked the story, but felt it was a little too graphic for his female readers, even though we all knew they didn't exist. Could he use it without the last line?

Without the last line, of course, there's no story. And I only reason I wrote the story a second time was so that I could re-use the last line. So I displayed artistic integrity I never knew I had and withdrew the story. I don't know what difference I thought it would make, since nobody read anything in that magazine anyway, but for once I just couldn't stop myself from doing the right thing. *Gallery* wound up taking it, last line and all. It was published as "Hot Eyes, Cold Eyes," and was later included in my second collection, *Like a Lamb to Slaughter*.

3. The title deserves explanation. Most of these stories were written in a single sitting. I would get an idea and sit down at the typewriter and hammer it out. You can hold a short-story idea entirely in the mind, especially the sort of brief and uncomplicated story that most of these are. A weekday evening or a weekend afternoon was generally time enough to see one of these stories through to the end.

It still often is. I still write stories rapidly, and sometimes complete one in a single setting. The major difference, it seems to me, is that the gestation period has gotten a lot longer. I'll nowadays let a story idea percolate or ferment or stew for days or weeks or months. Back then I tended to strike as soon as the iron was hot, or, occasionally, before it had really warmed up.

I've had three collections of short stories published, plus a small-press collection of the Ehrengraf stories and *Hit Man*, an episodic novel comprising the Keller stories. *One Night Stands* consists of stories deliberately omitted from these collections (or ones I'd lost track of, but if I'd had them handy I'd still have left them out).

What have we got here, then? A box labeled "pieces of string too small to save?" If they weren't worth collecting, why have I collected them?

IF MEMORY SERVES . . .

I've been guided by the same principle (or, some might argue, the same lack thereof) that has led me to republish some early crime novels that I'd be hard put to read without cringing. The fact that I can't read them with pleasure doesn't mean someone else couldn't, or shouldn't. I've decided it's not my job to judge my early work. Let other people make what they will of it.

Then too, I'm not unmindful of the interests of collectors and readers with a special interest in an author—in this instance, myself. I don't collect books, but I have other collecting interests, and I understand the mind set. Of course a collector would want a writer's early work, to read or simply to have and to hold, and why should I deprive him of the opportunity? And why shouldn't some scholar with a thesis to write have access to that early work?

At the same time, I don't think these stories are much good, or representative of my mature work. For God's sake, when I wrote these my typewriter still had training wheels on it. So I've decided *One Night Stands* should have limited distribution, going not to general readers but to collectors and specialists. Thus it's being published only in a limited collector edition, and not, as is generally the case with Crippen & Landru publications, in trade paperback as well.

Enough! This introduction has passed the 2500-word mark, which makes it longer than many of the stories it's introducing. It's taken most of the morning to write it, too. May you, Dear Reader. like the tomcat who had the affair with the skunk, enjoy these stories as much as you can stand.

                                            Lawrence Block
                                            Greenwich Village

THE BAD NIGHT

The shorter of the two-boys had wiry black hair and a twisted smile. He also had a knife, and the tip of the blade was pressed against Dan's faded gabardine jacket. "Why'd you have to get in the way?" he asked, softly. "Every bull from here to Memphis is after us, and Pops here has to . . ."

"Shut up." The older boy was taller, with blond hair that tumbled over his forehead. He, too, had a knife.

"Why? He ain't going to tell anybody. . ."

"Shut up, Benny." He turned to Dan, smiling. "We need money, maybe some food. We better make it over to your shack."

"No shack," Dan said. He gestured toward an opening in the wall of rock that edged the valley. "I live in the cave over there."

Benny started to laugh, and the blade of his knife pierced Dan's skin and drew blood. "A cave!" he exploded. "Dig, Zeke—he's a hermit!"

Zeke didn't laugh. "C'mon," he said. "To the cave."

They walked slowly across the field toward the mouth of the cave. Dan felt the sweat forming on his forehead, felt the old familiar sensation that he hadn't felt since Korea. He was afraid, as afraid as he'd ever been in his life.

"Faster," Benny said, and again Dan felt the knife prick skin. It didn't make sense. He'd lived through a world war and a police action, and now two kids from Memphis were going to kill him. Two kids who called him "Pops."

The veins stood out on his temples, and he could feel the sweat running down his face to the stubble of beard on his chin. "Why did he get in the way?" the kid had asked. Hell, he didn't mean to get in anyone's way. Just wanted to go off by himself, fool around with a little prospecting, and relax for awhile.

ONE NIGHT STANDS

They were almost at the entrance of the cave. Now they would take his money, eat his food, and put a switchblade knife between his ribs. He was finished, unless he managed to get to his gun in time. There was a shiny black .45 waiting on his shelf, if only he could get to it before Benny got to him with the knife.

"Here it is," he said. He stepped inside the cave, the two boys right behind him. It was a large cave, wide and roomy and branching out much wider in the rear. On one side was his mattress, on the other his trunk and four orange-crate shelves.

"Let's go," I said Zeke. "Bring out the dough and some food. We ain't got all night."

"Yeah," Benny echoed. "We gotta roll, man. Make it fast or I stick you, dig?" He prodded Dan with a knife for emphasis.

"Wait a minute." Dan's eyes darted desperately to the crates and lighted on the kerosene lantern. "Let me light the lamp over there. It's getting kind of dark in here."

Benny looked at Zeke, who shrugged. "Okay," he said. "But don't try anything." Dan walked across to the side of the cave, and Benny followed with the knife.

Fumbling in his pocket for a match, Dan glanced down to the middle shelf of the crate where the gun nestled cozily amidst a packet of letters and a pair of socks. If only he could get it, and if only it were loaded. Was it loaded? He couldn't remember.

"Hurry it up," Zeke said. It was now or never, Dan thought. He lifted the pack of matches from his pocket, tensed his body, and fell forward.

At the same time he lashed out viciously with his foot and heard a dull grunt of pain as he connected solidly with Benny's belly. His right hand snaked out for the gun and closed around it, his fingers caressing the smooth metal of the butt. All in one motion he took it and whirled around, his finger tight against the trigger. The boys scampered for the rear of the cave. Then, before he could get a shot off, his right ankle buckled and he fell to the floor. For a moment

THE BAD NIGHT

everything went black as the pain shot up and down his leg. He gritted his teeth until the floor stopped spinning.

Dan glanced around the cave, and the two boys seemed to have disappeared. He tried to stand, but the stab of pain in his ankle told him it was useless. The ankle was broken.

He could hear Zeke, cursing dully from the back of the cave. They hadn't left, then. He had them trapped.

After a time the cursing stopped. "Hey, Pops!" Zeke called. "That was pretty sharp, you know?"

Dan didn't answer.

"Sharp," the boy repeated. "You faked us good, but what'll it get you? You can't move, Pops."

Dan started. He scrutinized the rear walls of the cave but could see nothing.

"Peek-a-boo," Zeke called. "I can see you real good, Pops. There's a cool little crack in the rock, you know? I can see you clear as anything. You still got your gun, but you can't go anywhere."

"Neither can you," Dan answered, in spite of himself. "You can't come out without getting shot. You two little bastards can stay there until I get some help."

The boy's laugh rang hollowly in the cave. "Help? You expecting company, Pops? Bet there's a whole mess of people in a real rush to come here. This cave's a big attraction, huh?"

Dan ran a hand over his forehead. The boy was right—the world didn't exactly beat a path to his door. Daley would drop up in the morning with the mail, but he couldn't figure on anyone showing before then. It was a stalemate; he couldn't get the boys, and they couldn't get him.

"I can wait," he called. "My friend comes up at eleven every morning, and we can just sit it out until then. Have a nice wait, kids. Enjoy yourselves. When the cops get hold of you it won't be much fun."

This time they both laughed—high, shrill laughs that chilled Dan to the bone. The laughter echoed and bounced between the walls, and

ONE NIGHT STANDS

Dan felt his blood come to a boil. "Laugh!" he yelled, savagely. "Laugh your heads off, you little bastards!"

"Pops," called a voice—Benny's, this time. "The laugh's on you, Pops. Know what time it is?"

"It's nine o'clock, Pops. Nine at night. It's fourteen hours 'til your friend comes. Think you can stay awake for fourteen hours? That's a long time, you know."

Dan drew in a breath sharply. Suddenly, he felt very tired. Very tired and hopelessly old.

"He's right," Zeke said. "There's two of us, Pops, and we still got our blades. You might get real sleepy tonight. Just have to sit there all night with your eyes wide open, while one of us sleeps and the other one watches you. After awhile your eyes'll close up and that'll be the end. You'll be too sleepy to feel the knife."

The boy went on, but Dan didn't listen to the rest. He let out his breath slowly and stared at the gun in his hand, wondering idly whether or not it was loaded.

He knew what happened when a man had to force himself to stay awake. He'd seen a sentry who fell asleep it his post six miles north of Inchon. He'd looked like a man asleep, until Dan had noticed the slit that ran across his throat from ear to ear. He probably never knew what was happening, never felt the knife slice his life away.

Could he stay awake? He didn't know. He glanced at his watch, noting that the boy had been right—it was just a few minutes past nine. He'd been on his feet all day since 8:30 in the morning, and it had been a rough day, with plenty of walking and climbing. He felt tired already, and he had fourteen more hours to go. His ankle throbbed dully but steadily, a slow and persistent ache. He knew it was draining him of the energy he would need to remain awake through the night.

"You may not have to wait until you fall asleep," Zeke called. "It's getting real dark, man. You won't be able to see too good. We can sneak up, like."

THE BAD NIGHT

Dan looked around for the lantern and was relieved to find it at his side, where it had fallen in the scuffle. He set it upright and made ready to light it, then realized how little kerosene he had in it. Probably not enough to last the night. He'd save it until he couldn't see without it.

"Okay," said Zeke. "So you got the lamp. You'll still fall asleep."

The minutes crawled by and the shadows grew longer. Dan sat very still on the floor of the cave. The boys talked among themselves, and occasionally he caught snatches of their conversation. They'd started in Memphis, headed west, pulled a series of small hold-ups, and one of them—Benny, he guessed—had knifed the proprietor of a delicatessen. The man had died.

Killers. A couple of punk kids, but they had killed already and they would kill again. Zeke, he thought, would kill if he had to, but Benny was a different sort. Benny would kill whenever he got the chance.

Dan had met that kind before. There was a guy in his platoon, a tall, lean boy from the hills. And one day the platoon had taken seven young Chinese as prisoners. And the tall, lean boy from the hills had stepped up to each of the POWs in turn, and placed his pistol to the back of each head, quickly and methodically blowing out the brains of each of them. The Americans were too dumbfounded to stop him. Dan had been violently sick, and the memory still churned inside him.

He shook himself suddenly and took several deep breaths in rapid succession. He had almost fallen asleep that time. His eyes remained open, but his arms and legs were completely relaxed. He had heard about that—falling asleep bit by bit, until your mind wandered into dream-channels that seemed vividly real. He moved his arms around to speed the circulation and touched his injured ankle gingerly. It was sore to the touch and swelling rapidly.

ONE NIGHT STANDS

There was a laugh from the rear of the cave. "Almost," said Zeke. "You're an old man, Pops. Pretty soon you'll be dropping the gun. Why don't you just give it up?"

Damn you, thought Dan. He looked at his watch—10:20. It was dark now inside the cave, too dark for him to make out the outline of the rear wall. He'd have to chance running out of kerosene.

He struck a match and lit the lantern, warming his hands over it. It felt good. He hefted the gun in his hand. Was there a bullet left? The gun was full three days ago, but he had shot at some squirrels since then. How many times had he fired it? Five? Six? He couldn't remember.

Nor was it possible to tell by the weight. He could judge between a full gun and an empty one, but one bullet either way didn't make that much of a difference.

He noticed himself blinking more and more frequently, as his eyes struggled to shut against his will. He forced himself to look first at the lantern, then off into the darkened area of the cave. *Just so it isn't steady,* he thought. *Vary it, mix it up, just so you don't get accustomed to one position.* He moved his arms from time to time, shifted his weight, and changed the position of his legs as much as the broken ankle would permit.

The boys spoke less, then stopped talking altogether. It was almost midnight when he heard Zeke's voice, soft but clear in the near-silence of the night.

"Pops," the boy said, "Benny's sleeping. Isn't that nice?"

He didn't answer. There was no point in wasting energy; he needed every drop of it just to keep awake.

"I said he's asleep," the boy repeated. "Just closed his eyes and floated right off. Sleeping like a baby."

Stop it, Dan thought fiercely. *Don't talk about it, you bastard. Don't even mention the word.*

But Zeke knew what he was doing. "Sleeping. Wouldn't you like to take a little nap right now, Pops? Be real easy, you know? Just close your eyes, lean back . . ."

20

THE BAD NIGHT

No. His hand tightened on the butt of the gun, squeezing hard. He started to sweat again, and then a cold chill came over him.

"Relax," the voice cooed. "You're real tired. You want to catch a little sleep. Close your eyes. Go ahead—close them."

Dan's eyelids dropped by themselves at the command, and he had to struggle to lift them again. He was being hypnotized, crudely but efficiently.

"Damn you!" he roared. *"God Damn you!"* The boy chuckled. Zeke's chuckle grew into a laugh, and Dan could feel his pulse racing. He shouldn't have blown up. He had to relax, had to take things slowly and easily.

Zeke began again, slowly and methodically urging him to sleep, but Dan forced his mind to ignore the suggestions. It wasn't easy.

His body was beginning to rebel as he alternately sweated and shivered. His ankle ached with a vengeance until he wanted to put a bullet through it. But for all he knew the gun was empty. He didn't dare break it open to check. Zeke was watching him constantly, commenting on every move he made. If the gun *was* empty. . .

He began glancing at his watch with increasing frequency. It seemed as though time was standing still for him, as though he and the two devils were suspended in a stalemate for eternity. But the weight of his eyelids and the nagging aches of his body assured him that this was not the case. He grew weaker and more tired with each passing second.

A few minutes past one, his grip relaxed and the gun nearly dropped from his hand. He swore and the boy laughed.

Is it loaded? Dammit, is it loaded? And then, suddenly, *what the hell difference does it make?*

He realized that it made no difference at all. Whether the gun was empty or full, they *thought* it was full. And because they thought he held a loaded gun, they were waiting for him to fall asleep. As long as . . .

"Pops," the voice interrupted him, "Zeke's gonna have a little nap. Ain't he lucky?"

ONE NIGHT STANDS

Shut up.

"You'll be sleeping soon, Pops. Then I'll have a chance to cut you good. Dig?" Benny had none of the hypnotic effect of Zeke, but his words dug at Dan's brain and broke his train of thought.

Dan clenched his hands into fists and bit his lip so hard that he tasted blood in his mouth. If they *thought* he was awake, and that the gun was loaded, they wouldn't approach him. The real thing didn't matter. It was what they thought.

"I don't think I'll give it to you quick, Pops. I'll just take that gun away and do a nice slow job. Think you'll like that? I'm good with a blade. Real good."

Now how could he sleep, yet make them think he was awake? They could watch him clearly, watch the eyes shut and the gun fall. His fingers would relax, so slowly that he wouldn't ever feel it, and the gun would slip, gently to the floor. How could he fake it?

"Think you're tough, Pops? You won't be so tough. I'll cut you up *so* slow. You'll bawl, you know? A big guy like you, you'll bawl like a baby."

Of course, he could put out the lantern. Then they couldn't see whether or not he slept. He reached for the lantern, then hesitated. It wouldn't work.

Without the lantern, he wouldn't be able to see them either. They could sneak up, just as Zeke had suggested. And he knew that he would never be able to stay awake in the darkness. He'd fall asleep within minutes.

"Go to sleep, Pops. Go to sleep, you rotten bastard."

Dan blinked rapidly and sucked in a large mouthful of air. Time was passing, and it was on their side. But . . . and suddenly he had it! As soon as he fell asleep, they would know it. And he would fall asleep before help came. But if they *thought* he was asleep. Just like the gun, the truth of the picture didn't matter.

For the next five minutes he sat very still, scarcely moving at all. Then, slowly and carefully, he let his eyelids drop shut. He breathed deeply and rhythmically. He relaxed.

THE BAD NIGHT

Benny's taunts had ceased, and he could bear the boy's quiet breathing at the rear of the cave. Slowly, bit by bit, he let his fingers relax and his fist open, until the gun dropped from his grip and bounced gently upon the earth.

Minutes passed. Then he heard movement at the rear of the cave, followed by the clean, metallic *click* of the switchblade knife. They would be coming soon. He kept his eyes closed and his breathing regular.

A hushed whisper, followed by more movement and another click, informed him that Zeke was also awake. He waited, tense as a drum. His left arm began to itch insistently, but he didn't even consider scratching it. He let it itch and bit harder on his lip until the blood came.

There was more movement. He was able to sense, even with his eyes closed, that they stood in plain sight of him now. He could see them clearly in his mind—Zeke cautious, expressionless; Benny anxious, his eyes gleaming.

Here they come. You can even hear them breathing. They're getting closer, and you only get one chance. Get ready...

Now!

In one movement he snapped open his eyes and grabbed for the gun. They were barely ten feet away, rooted in their tracks as he came to life before their eyes. He raised the gun, hooked his finger around the trigger, and leveled it at Zeke's chest.

"Drop 'em," he said. "Drop the knives."

Benny gaped like a fish. His hand trembled and the knife fell to the earth.

"Now you," Dan ordered. "Drop it!"

There was no smile on Zeke's face now. The dead-pan expression was gone, too, and fear mingled with surprise replaced it. He dropped the knife.

"Now kick them across the floor." They did as he said.

ONE NIGHT STANDS

He let out a breath, finally. "Okay," he said. "Now, you both lie down on your bellies, facing me. Zeke, you start crawling over here. Benny, you better stay right where you are."

Zeke inched his way forward. When he was within reach, Dan chopped him viciously across the head with the barrel of the gun. "Go to sleep," he said. "Pleasant dreams, fella."

He lifted the gun and pointed it at Benny. "Now you," he snapped. "Get over here."

"No! Please!"

"Maybe you want a bullet instead, Benny? This is a big gun, you know? Makes a big hole."

Benny didn't say anything.

"Get over here!"

The first swipe of the gun barrel knocked Benny unconscious. Dan hit him again, anyway.

He worked quickly. He tore their clothing into strips and bound their ankles and wrists securely. They'd be unable to get loose for a good long while. Long before then Daley would arrive with the mail, and that would be that.

Dan settled back, turned out the lamp, and went to sleep.

THE BADGER GAME

Baron followed the bellhop from the elevator to the room. The bellhop opened the door for him and followed him inside, depositing the single brown leather suitcase on the floor. His hand was ready at once to accept the crisp dollar bill Baron handed to him.

"Will there be anything else, sir?" The boy's eyes indicated that "anything else" took in a wide range of possible services.

Baron considered. A woman might be pleasant, but there would be plenty of time for that later. Besides, he liked to take what he wanted without paying for it.

He dismissed the bellhop with a curt shake of his head and turned away from him. When the door closed behind the boy he kicked off his shoes and stretched out full-length upon the bed.

Richard Baron did not look like a criminal. His clothes were expensive without being flashy—his shoes were black Italian loafers that had cost him thirty dollars a pair and the grey flannel suit cut in the latest continental style had set him back a little over two hundred. His shirts were all white-on-white and had been made to his measurements.

The average Joe would have pegged him for a successful young businessman from the West Coast. Somebody with a little more on the ball might have made him for a hustler in the Organization—not a muscle boy, but somebody with an angle.

Baron was a con man.

It was, he reflected, a good life. For the moment he had nothing to do but relax, and it wasn't hard to relax with a full wallet and $15,000 in his suitcase, fifteen grand in tens and twenties that he could spend whenever he got around to it. The oil man in Dallas hadn't stopped payment on his check and wouldn't even think of it.

ONE NIGHT STANDS

The oil man now thought he was the owner of several hundred acres of Canada loaded with uranium. As it happened, the oil man now owned a few hundred totally worthless stock certificates. By the time he found out he had been taken, he wouldn't even remember what Baron looked like.

The oil man had put up a little over $75,000. Baron's end of the deal was twenty grand, and it would take awhile to spend it. Not as long as it might take most people, because Baron liked to live somewhat better than most people did. The better restaurants, the better nightclubs, and the better women all helped lift his life to a higher plain. He drank nothing but Jack Daniels and ate nothing but blood-rare steak.

Actually, expensive living was essential in his occupation. It seems as though marks would only permit themselves to be swindled by men who appeared to be rich. A threadbare pin-stripe might do for a sneak thief, but a confidence man had to come on strong if he wanted to score.

Now he could bide his time. Tulsa wasn't exactly the place he would choose for a vacation, but the telegram from Lou Farmer had indicated that Lou had a mark hanging fire in Denver that might be ripe any day. A trip to Miami or New York was out until the mark fell one way or the other.

Baron hauled himself up from the bed and stripped for a shower. He was thirty-five but in better physical shape than when he'd been twenty and working the short con in railway stations, grifting hard for ten bucks here and twenty bucks there.

He'd come a long way in fifteen years. A grifter's money went quickly, but Baron had a growing bank account in New York and a healthy stack of dough in the stock market. Not in the kind of wild moose pasture that he sold to the marks, but a solid mutual fund that grew steadily and paid a nice dividend. A few more heavy scores and he'd be able to lay off for the rest of his life.

He toweled himself dry after the shower and shaved with a straight razor, applying a few drops of after-shaving lotion and a few

THE BADGER GAME

more of an expensive cologne that he liked. He dressed again, changing to a pair of charcoal slacks and a light brown cashmere sport jacket.

He locked the suitcase and left it in the closet, not really worried that the lock would be broken. It didn't matter if it was; the money was snug in the case's false bottom.

It was too early for dinner and he walked leisurely through downtown Tulsa. It was amazing, he thought to himself, the way the average guy never noticed what was happening. He spotted a cannon mob grifting the other side of the street, working their way through the pockets of passing shoppers. Baron picked out the hook easily and watched him work, dipping easily into a mark's back pocket and passing the wallet to one of the other members of the mob in a second. Smooth.

Just for the hell of it he crossed the street at the end of the block and doubled back the other way. The cannons were moving toward him and he let one of the prat men bump him gently while he pretended to study the display in a shoe store. Only because he was concentrating was he able to feel the wire's hand dip into his pocket, reaching for his wallet.

Baron said: "Nix."

He half-whispered the word so that nobody but the wire would hear it. But the wire got the message. Instantly the hand was withdrawn and the wallet remained where it was.

Baron smiled to himself and moved on. Again the prat man jostled him, this time mumbling "sorry" under his breath. Baron's smile widened. The thief was indicating he was sorry he had made Baron for a mark.

It was always a source of pleasure to him the way a thief could communicate to another thief without a mark ever catching on. He and Farmer and the others in his outfit could talk over the head of a mark forever. And just the one word, "nix," had put the cannon mob wise to who he was.

ONE NIGHT STANDS

Baron glanced at his watch. It was 6:30 now and he was hungry. He walked to the curb and caught a cab.

"Take me to the best steakhouse in town," he told the driver.

At the restaurant he had a double shot of Jack Daniels on the rocks and a rare sirloin an inch and a half thick. He finished off with a pony of drambuie, inhaling the rich vapor of the cordial and enjoying the warm feeling as it trailed down his throat to his stomach. He paid the check and tipped the waiter generously.

He bought a paper at a corner news-stand and glanced at the entertainment page. There were only a few nightclubs in Tulsa and none of them seemed particularly appealing. How would he spend the evening?

A woman would be pleasant. He considered taking the bellhop up on his offer but gave up the idea. Later, perhaps, but not tonight.

Instead he caught a cab back to his hotel and wandered into the bar. He'd just have a few drinks and then catch a full night's sleep. If there was a woman to be picked up he would pick her up, and if there wasn't he wouldn't be too disappointed.

At the bar he took the furthest stool from the door and ordered a shot of Jack Daniels with a water chaser. He tossed off the shot and was lifting the glass of water to his lips when he spotted the blond.

He saw her before she saw him. She was tall, just a few inches shorter than he was. And her hair was long and golden. The plain black cocktail dress emphasized her high, full breasts and her long, tapered legs.

Her face was good, too, except for a slightly hard look about it. Looks, he decided. Plenty of looks, but not a hell of a lot of class.

Automatically he wondered what angle she was working. She didn't come on like a hustler, but it was a cinch she was pushing her looks in one way or another. He sipped the chaser and waited for her to make her play.

He didn't have long to wait. Her eyes surveyed the room rapidly and she walked directly to him, taking the seat beside him. She

THE BADGER GAME

ordered a grasshopper and the bartender mixed the drink in a hurry and brought it to her.

Baron paid for her drink.

"Thanks," she said, smiling at him. "Are you with the convention?"

He shook his head. "I'm working the C out of Philly," he said, deciding to fill her in right away so she could save her time. If she was a pro she'd know enough to make her pitch straight instead of playing games; if she was in the rackets she would leave him alone.

She didn't seem to have heard him. "I came down with my husband for the convention," she said. "You know, the auto merchants are having this convention. It started yesterday."

He nodded briefly.

"My husband had this meeting tonight," she said. "He won't be back until one or two in the morning. It gets boring for a girl, just sitting alone in a room."

He smiled; she didn't waste her time. He made her grift at once — it had to be the badger game the way she was planting her story. She would take him to her room and then her husband would come on with a gun, pretending to be furious. The hubby would threaten to kill him and settle for a cash settlement, and that would be that.

But she wasn't being very smooth about it. She should pretend to be more reluctant and make him do a little more of the work. Otherwise the mark wouldn't swallow the bait whole.

"What's your name?"

"Dick Baron," he said. "I just got finished working the rag in Dallas." Now she would have to realize he was in the know.

But she seemed totally oblivious to what he had said.

"I'm lonely," she said. "And I've got a bottle up in my room. Would you like to come up with me?"

He almost broke out laughing. Now he had the whole picture. She was working the badger game, all right, but she wasn't a professional at it. That's why her approach was so lousy and why she

ONE NIGHT STANDS

was missing the lines he was throwing at her. She was a crook, but an amateur crook.

And if there was one thing Baron couldn't stand it was an amateur crook. They didn't know the ropes and all they did was make things rough for the smart boys. Here was this blond now, working like a slave to con a con man. How dumb could you get?

"Sure," he said, deciding to play along. "Let's go upstairs."

On the way to the elevator she took his arm, which was another mistake. She should let him do all the work—that way he'd believe she was a straight chick taking a first fling. It would make him hotter for her and at the same time scare him silly when her partner came on the scene.

"My name's Sally English," she said. "My husband and I are from Cedar Rapids."

He nodded and she tightened her grip on his arm. "I suppose you think I'm a tramp," she went on. "I'm not, not really. Don't you think I'm a tramp?"

"I think you're swell," he said, thinking that anybody who made such a mess out of a simple badger dodge ought to starve to death.

"I've never done this before," she said. "I mean, pick up somebody I never met before and take him to my room. But I get so lonely."

In the elevator she leaned against him and he could feel the warmth of her flesh through the thin cocktail dress. Hell, maybe he'd wind up making it with her if he played it right. She might be dumb, but she was certainly built for action. The top of her head was inches from his nose and he could smell her perfume. It was cheap stuff and she used a little too much of it. But there was no denying that it increased his desire for her.

Her room was on the floor beneath his. She led him inside and closed the door but didn't turn the lock, explaining that her husband couldn't possibly get home before one or two. Again, that was part of the pattern—but she shouldn't have bothered with the explanation. She was being too damned obvious about the whole thing.

30

THE BADGER GAME

She fished around in the dresser and came up with a fifth of blended rye, pouring tumblers full for each of them. He wondered idly whether she might be working it solo, planning on drugging him and picking his pocket. It was possible.

At any rate he had better things to do than swill cheap rye. When she wasn't looking he emptied his glass on the rug beneath the bed.

He slipped his arm around her and she turned to him, fastening her mouth on his. He kissed her and her tongue probed his mouth. Even if she played the rest of it wrong she knew what to do once she was in the bedroom, he decided. That one kiss had been enough to make him ache with desire for her.

Suddenly she stood up and reached behind her to unzip the dress. He stood up and helped, noting with approval that she wasn't wearing a bra. Everything under the dress was hers.

He had to draw in his breath. She had a superb body—firm and young and vibrantly alive.

He took a step toward her.

And then, right on schedule, a key turned in the lock, the door opened, and hubby walked in.

Baron was perfectly calm as he looked first at the man and then at the girl. The man should have had a gun; it would have made the situation more convincing. Outside of that the pair were effective actors. The girl was cringing against the wall. The man had fury blazing in his eyes and his hands were knotted into fists.

"Cut it," Baron snapped, suddenly angry at the amateur quality of the whole thing. "It doesn't work this time."

The man advanced on him, swearing.

Baron decided he had had just about enough of the whole thing. Besides, he wanted the girl, wanted her as he hadn't wanted a woman in a long time.

He meant to have her.

He met the man's rush neatly, blocking a punch and countering with a right to the chest. The man sagged and Baron chopped him savagely on the side of the neck.

ONE NIGHT STANDS

Such a chop, properly done, kills a man. Baron had killed a man in just such a fashion several years back when he had to play it heavy for a change. This time he held back slightly with the blow. The man crumpled to the floor, alive but unconscious. He would remain unconscious for at least twenty minutes.

Baron turned to the girl. She was cowering against the wall, her eyes wide with terror that was quite probably genuine.

He laughed.

"Didn't expect that, did you? You ought to learn to tell who's a mark and who isn't."

"Please," she said. "Please."

"This time," he said, "you're going to have to go through with it. Maybe you'll learn better next time."

He took her by the shoulders and heaved her toward the bed. She stumbled for a few steps and sat down heavily. She didn't move.

Back in his own room Baron felt thoroughly relaxed for the first time in weeks. Sally English—or whatever her name might really be—was more woman than he had had in quite a while. She had one hell of a body and she knew what to do with it.

Baron smiled, remembering and enjoying the memory. At first she had fought, but after awhile she quit fighting and started to enjoy what she was doing.

He laughed suddenly, wondering what the poor dope of a partner would think when he came to. The guy had been expecting a mark, not a guy who would knock him cold. It served him right for being such a damned amateur.

Well, maybe they would drop out of the rackets now. The badger game was a short con to begin with and not an especially good one at that, but that pair wasn't cut out for anything so professional. Maybe the girl would hustle and the guy would pimp for her. He decided that the guy wasn't much better than a pimp. And the girl would make a fine hustler.

THE BADGER GAME

Amateur crooks. They only got in the way, lousing things up for the boys who knew which end was up. They didn't know who to take and who to pass up.

And they always got caught. And when they got caught they didn't know what to do, and so they wound up in the tank. Which, Baron reflected, was precisely where they belonged, the whole pack of them.

The professionals got caught too—but they didn't wind up in jail, not the smart ones. When they hit a town they found out who was the fixer and they established contact with the fixer before they started grifting. That way they stayed out of the jug.

If they got busted they either bought the cop right away or got word to the fixer, who bought whoever had to be bought. Sometimes the fixer would get to the mark and pay him off to get him to drop charges. That was the way most of the cannon mobs operated. If that failed, the fixer bought the judge. Almost any judge would square a small rap for the right price.

But amateurs! If a mark turned in Sally and her partner they would be lost. They might have the brains to get a lawyer, but if they did they'd still wind up doing a year or two apiece. Because the same judge who could be bought would go extra hard on an amateur, just to keep his record looking good.

The hell with them, Baron thought. They deserved whatever happened to them.

Mentally he went over all the way the pair had played the game wrong. To begin with, Sally's whole approach was too heavy. She should have sat down a stool or two away from him instead of right next to him. She should have let him offer to buy her a drink—the second drink, not the first. She should have mentioned her husband right away and then left the rest of it up to Baron.

And, of course, she should have caught on to what he was talking about. The first words he spoke were, "I'm working the C out of Philly." This meant, quite simply, that he was a confidence man who started originally in Philadelphia. But she didn't even listen to him.

ONE NIGHT STANDS

Then, later, he had told her he had just finished pulling off a rag, a phony stock con. Anybody but a damn fool would have caught that.

And her "husband" was just as stupid. He should have knocked first, then used the key. He was supposed to be expecting to find her in, so why in the hell didn't he knock? And he should have had a gun. Not loaded, of course. Not even a real gun, if he wanted to play extra safe. But as soon as he came in swinging he was making things hard for himself. Hell, even a mark might have gotten lucky and clipped him one.

Well, that was all over. In a day or two he'd get a wire from Lou and head either for Denver or the coast. And he would have happy memories of Tulsa.

There was a knock on the door.

Baron swung himself off the bed, wondering who was at the door. Maybe the telegram, he thought. Or maybe Sally, back for another round.

He walked to the door and opened it.

The "husband" was at the door. There was a gun in his hand.

"Inside," the man said. "Get inside."

Baron backed up, puzzled. The man followed him and closed the door behind him.

"Look," Baron said, "go home. You made me for a mark and you missed. Quit while you're ahead."

The man said, "I'm going to kill you."

"You tried to cop a score and you blew it."

The man's eyes were blazing. "I don't know what you're talking about," he said. "All I know is you were with my wife. I just finished beating the crap out of her. She won't be able to walk for a month. Now I'm going to kill you."

Baron just looked at him.

"She told me she was going to the movies," he went on dully. "I come back and she's with you. I always knew she was a tramp. I had to knock her silly before she'd tell me your name. And I had to give the clerk five bucks before he'd give me your room number."

34

THE BADGER GAME

"Now I'm going to kill you."

Baron started to laugh. No wonder their approach was so amateurish!

The man pointed the gun at him. Baron laughed again, thinking that it was really no time to laugh. But what the hell else could he do?

The man pulled the trigger.

Baron sat down heavily on the bed and began laughing once more. He couldn't help it. In a few seconds he stopped laughing because he was dead.

BARGAIN IN BLOOD

"You've got to prove it to me," she said.

He puffed nervously on his cigarette before answering her. She was a very beautiful girl, very well put together and very desirable, and it wasn't often that a girl like this even bothered to talk to him. He had to be very careful; he didn't want to say the wrong thing and maybe spoil everything before it even got off the ground.

"How do you mean?"

She took the cigarette from his fingers and dragged deeply on it. "You know," she said, talking through the smoke. "You say you want me, right?"

"Right."

"That's important, Benny. A guy's got to want me or he doesn't get me. Dig?"

He nodded. He wanted her, all right. He wanted her from the first time he saw her, before he even knew her name. He wanted her so much sometimes that he couldn't sleep and just lay in bed thinking about her, thinking about the way her blond hair curled around her face and the way her body could twist a sweater out of shape.

All the time he thought about her, but he never expected to get her. Not him. Not Benny Dix, the little kid with the pimples. The little kid with no dough and no car to drive around in, the little kid nobody paid much attention to at all.

She had class and he didn't; it was that simple. She was the type of chick who went with an important cat, a cat maybe like Moe. But she wasn't going with Moe now. She and Moe split, and now she was there for Benny. Maybe it didn't make sense, but it was nice. Real nice. She was so close to him now that he could reach out and touch her, and there was nobody else around the park, nobody to bother them.

BARGAIN IN BLOOD

"If you want me," she went on, "you got to show it. I need proof, Benny. You know why I broke with Moe?"

"Why?"

"No proof. Moe wanted me, but not enough to let me know it. You probably thought Moe was making it with me, didn't you?"

"I—"

"It's okay. Everybody thought so, but he wasn't. Not Moe or anybody else in this jerkwater town. Not because I'm cold, because I can be hot as a Nathan's hot dog for the right cat. But because I need proof. I could be hot for you, Benny."

He felt his hands starting to shake and struggled to control them. He'd give her the proof, whatever the hell it was. It didn't matter: he had to have her, and that was all there was to it.

"What kind of proof?" His voice sounded hollow to him, hollow and nervous and tense, like when he was playing chickie and a cop car passed right by the hardware store, and then the cop car slowed down and he didn't know what to do, whether he should holler chickie or just wait for the cops to take off. Then the cops stepped on the gas and disappeared, and that came out the right way.

She was looking at him now, her eyes drilling holes in his, studying him very carefully. There was something so intense and direct about her gaze that he wanted to turn away, as if she were staring at him the way he did when he undressed a girl with his eyes. But this was deeper—she was undressing his insides, trying to decide about him.

"I want you to kill somebody."

"What?"

She smiled. "That's right, Benny. You heard me right. I want you to take a blade and slip it right into a cat's guts, understand? That's the kind of proof I want."

"Why, Rita? I mean—"

"To prove it. I'm nice stuff, Benny. I'm not easy, and I'll be worth it. Then we can do whatever you want whenever you want to."

ONE NIGHT STANDS

His mind was racing in circles. He knew she was telling the truth. She'd be worth it, worth almost anything. But killing a guy was a big thing. If they caught you, you burned. And it wasn't like knocking over a candy store—they tried harder to catch you for murder.

Murder.

"Who's the cat? Anybody special?"

"You mean you'll do it?"

"Wait a minute. I just want to know who, that's all."

She took a breath. "Moe," she said.

"Moe?"

"That's right. You slip the shank in Moe and it's just you and me, Benny, for as long as you want it. What do you say?"

This was big. It was big enough shanking someone he didn't know, bad enough to slip steel into a cat he never met. But Moe was worse. Hell, he wasn't tight with Moe and he wouldn't miss him, not Moe with the short car with wire wheels and a girl in the backseat whenever he wanted one. No, he could see Moe dead without crying about it. But killing him—

"It'll be easy," she went on, her voice husky and all excited. "It's about 9:30 now. I can go to his pad and pick him up. I'll tell him some lies so he thinks he's getting something now. Then we'll come walking over towards the park and you can get him about ten steps inside the North Entrance. Okay?"

He turned a little on the bench, looking off into the distance. He was shook now. Killing— He couldn't pull a bit like that, not him.

And then he felt her small hand on his thigh.

"Okay," he said.

He saw them coming a long ways off. He heard them before he saw them, heard Moe's low, relaxed voice and Rita's, tense and shrill with anticipation. When they came into view he saw Moe's arm around her slender waist, his hand gently squeezing her flesh.

It made him mad, and he knew he'd be able to do it. He'd get even with Moe. He'd get even with him for all the girls he never had and the money he was never able to toss around.

BARGAIN IN BLOOD

They came closer. He took his knife from his dungarees pocket and clicked it open, fearing for a moment that Moe would hear the click of the blade and know what was going to happen. But Moe didn't notice. It was no wonder—Rita was leaning against him as they walked, and it would be tough for a cat to notice anything with a girl like her doing the leaning.

He rubbed his thumb nervously over the blade, feeling how sharp it was and wondering how it would go into Moe. It would go in nice and smooth, he decided. One push and that would be the end of Moe. And that little push would also serve as the beginning of Benny Dix.

They entered the park and stopped. They were just steps from him now, just steps from him and the knife and the murder. It was time now. He knew this, but he couldn't force himself to move for a moment, as if he were made of wood.

Now.

He stepped out from behind the tree and closed the gap between them in three quick strides, impatient to get it all over with as quickly as possible. Moe looked up and saw him, and he saw the total surprise in his eyes and the excitement and joy in Rita's. Then the expression in Moe's eyes changed to fear when he saw the knife, and he started to move but he couldn't move fast enough, couldn't dodge the knife that was coming up toward his soft belly, couldn't even scream when the knife went in and up into him, could only clutch at his gut as he fell back and crumpled to the pavement.

Rita came to him and stood next to him, and his arm went around her while she looked down at the body that a few minutes ago had been Moe. She was breathing hard now, hot and excited, staring as if she were hypnotized at the pool of blood below her. The blood looked almost purple in the light of the moon.

They stood in their tracks for several moments without either of them moving or saying a word. He felt torn in half, sick at the realization that Moe was dead and he had killed him, and hungry for Rita and knowing that he was going to get her now, that the

ONE NIGHT STANDS

loneliness and emptiness was over from here on in. She had the proof she wanted.

"Come on," she said at last. "Let's get out of here."

"Where to?"

"My pad. The folks are away for the weekend and nobody's going to bother us. You think you'll like that, Benny?"

"Yeah." His voice was hoarse and tight.

She slipped her hand in his and gave it a squeeze as they started walking swiftly out of the park. "I think you will, too," she said. "I think we'll both have a good time."

"Give me the knife," she said. I'll wash it up so nobody can prove anything, okay?" She took the knife and walked off into the bathroom, and he kicked off his shoes and lay down on the bed to wait for her. He hadn't felt this way in a long time—wanting something so much that it was an ache instead of an ordinary hunger, and at the same time knowing that now he was going to get what he wanted, that she was in the next room and soon she would be in the same room with him, lying down on the bed beside him, and then he would have her.

Moe was dead. He killed Moe, but nobody was going to suspect him and no cops were going to prove anything even if they did figure it all out. Moe was dead in the park and he was in Rita's bed waiting for her, and even if killing was a bad thing there was nothing to do about it. It was all over—besides, it had to happen just the way it happened. He couldn't help it, not at all.

She was running water in the bathroom, washing the knife. Smart girl, he thought. The chick would figure all the angles. If the cops made noises, she could tell how the two of them were together all the time. It was clear.

She came back holding the knife in her hand and set it down on the little brown table at the head of the bed. "It's clean," she explained. "I'm leaving it open for now so it'll dry out, but there's no sweat now. Nobody saw a thing."

BARGAIN IN BLOOD

He nodded, and she sat down on the bed and kicked off her shoes. "You did it," she said. "You proved it to me, Benny. I knew you'd have the guts, and I knew you wanted me bad enough. That was the important part."

He didn't answer. She leaned back on the bed, resting her head on the pillow beside his. He could smell her perfume and the fragrance of her hair and he wanted to reach for her and take her right away without waiting for anything. He'd been with chicks before, but never one like Rita, never one who was made for this sort of thing, one that oozed sex with every step she took.

It was going to be good.

"I want you, too." She moved even closer to him and he turned so that their bodies pressed together tightly. He could feel every contour of her body and his arms went around her quickly, and then they were kissing. His heart was beating wildly and he couldn't control his breathing and he was no longer conscious of the room or the bed or the naked light-bulb hanging over the bed or the knife on the night-table.

He was only conscious of his body and hers and nothing else mattered at all.

When it was over he lay motionless on the bed while she sat up and rearranged her clothing. He felt complete now for the first time in a long time, complete and whole and relaxed at last. She was even better than she'd promised, better than he had imagined.

He could almost forget Moe and the sick expression on his face when the knife tore into his stomach. Moe was something that couldn't be avoided, something in the way that had to be removed. It wasn't his fault for killing Moe, any more than it was his fault for being born or wanting Rita. It just happened that way.

And it was good for her, too. She loved every minute of it, every second of the act. From here on in to was peaches and cream for Benny Dix, with Rita whenever he wanted her. And he would want plenty.

"You liked it," he said. "Didn't you?"

ONE NIGHT STANDS

"Of course. Couldn't you tell?" There was a touch of amusement in her voice, a note of her knowing something that he was missing.

"Yeah. I mean— You like doing that. You like it every time, don't you?"

"Uh-huh."

Well, he'd give her plenty to like. He rolled over on one elbow and looked at her, sitting silently on the edge of the bed. She looked even prettier than before and it was hard to believe that he had actually made love to her, that he had scored with such a good looking-broad. But he could believe it. He could remember every second of it as if it were still happening.

"I bet there's nothing you like better," he went on, talking slowly. "You proved that you wanted me, just like I proved it to you. Right?"

She nodded, and he could just make out the shadow of a smile on her face.

"That's what I figured. A guy can tell if a chick's faking, you know?"

"I wasn't faking."

"You don't have to tell me. You must like it better than anything else in the world."

The smile grew wider. "Almost," she said, softly. "There's only one thing in the world I like better, Benny. Just one thing." As she spoke, it seemed to him as though she were playing some kind of a game with him.

"Yeah?" he said, mildly curious. "What's that?"

"Something I just saw," she answered, and he still didn't know what she was talking about. "It was fun to see it, Benny, and I bet it's even better when you do it yourself!"

He opened his mouth to say something, and his mouth remained uselessly open as he saw the knife in her hand, the knife he had used on Moe. For one brief second he saw the answer to his question in her eyes; for one instant he knew what she really craved, what kind of excitement sent her blood racing. Just for that single second when

BARGAIN IN BLOOD

he watched the insane stare in her eyes as she gazed at the blood gushing from the stab-wound in his chest.

A second later his vision blurred and he saw nothing.

In another second he was dead.

BRIDE OF VIOLENCE

She didn't say a word when I pulled the car off the road behind the clump of young poplars. I cut the motor and flicked off the lights. Then I pulled her to me and kissed her.

The kiss sent my blood. racing. This was nothing new. Just being with Rita, just looking at her and running my eyes over the full curves of her body enough to send me it a sweat

I forced myself to pull away from her. "Come on," I said. "Let's get into the back seat."

She smiled, teasing me. "Why?"

"You know why."

"Tell me anyway."

I just looked at her. Her hair was long and golden and it spilled over her shoulders like a yellow waterfall. Her mouth was red with the lipstick I hadn't managed to kiss away yet. Her eyes were a sort of cornflower blue that deepened almost to purple in the dark.

I wanted her so much it was killing me.

"Quit playing games," I said.

"Games?" The eyes widened.

"Come on."

She smiled. "I just want you to tell I me why we should get in the back seat, Jim. That's all."

"Don't you know?"

"I'm not sure," she said. "Maybe you have designs on my virtue. How should I know?"

"Rita—"

"Her face softened. "I'm sorry, Jim," she said. "I don't like to tease you."

Not much, I thought. I didn't say anything.

BRIDE OF VIOLENCE

"It's just that I don't want us to get too involved, Jim. Honey, every time we park the car and neck up a storm we go a little farther than we did last time. I'm afraid sometime we won't be able to stop."

"What's wrong if we don't"

"Jim—"

"Well what if we don't? God, Rita, I want you and you want me and that ought to be enough. Why in hell won't you let me make love to you?"

"I've already told you that."

"But it doesn't make any sense!"

She moved closer to me I could feel her breasts pressing against my chest. My skin felt warm beneath my shirt where she was touching me. Her lips brushed my cheek."

"Not until we're married," she said. "I've told you a dozen times, darling."

More than a dozen times, I thought. *Closer to a hundred times*. I kissed her again, almost absently, thinking that this was just a repeat of a conversation the two of us went through almost every night.

But I had to keep going.

"We're going to be married," I said, "as soon as I get enough money saved up so that we won't have to pick through garbage cans when we want breakfast."

"I know."

"I'd marry you now," I went on. "Waiting was your idea, Rita. I—"

"You know it's the only sensible thing to do." She was closer to me now, so close I could feel every outline of her warm body. My arm slipped around her and stroked the firm flesh. I had a hard time getting the next sentence out; I wasn't much in the mood for conversation.

"Okay," I said. "Waiting to get married is sensible. But waiting to make love isn't."

"Suppose I got pregnant?" she demanded.

ONE NIGHT STANDS

The same old arguments every damned night. "You won't," I said.

"You can't be sure about that, Jim. It happens, you know."

"Then we'd get married right away."

"And then we'd have everybody counting the months and snickering when the baby was born. I don't want that, Jim."

I didn't answer.

"But that's not the main thing. I'm an old-fashioned girl, honey. I want to wait until I'm married. That's all there is to it."

She seemed to be right—that was all there was to it. That was the trouble.

She snuggled up to me again. "I don't really feel like talking," she said. "Do you?"

"No," I said. "Of course not."

"We'll wait then? Until we're married?"

I nodded.

"Okay," she said. "Then let's get in the back seat."

I opened the door and helped her out and into the backseat. Then I reached for her and she came to me and our mouths met as they always did—hot and hungry and demanding. I kissed her again, savagely.

She purred like a kitten.

Then I was undoing the buttons on her blouse, and my arms were around her. I pressed her close to me and kissed her. My hands caressing her sift flesh. I fumbled with the catches of her bra.

"Here," she said. "Let me do that."

She broke away and reached behind her and the motion made her firm breasts strain against the bra until I thought it would break. Then the bra was off and she was in my arms again.

"Rita," I said. "God, I love you."

"She started to say something but I stopped her mouth with mine. I held her and stroked her and kissed her and watched her turn from a beautiful girl into a hungry, passionate woman in my arms, her eyes burning like purple fires into mine.

BRIDE OF VIOLENCE

Then I slipped my hand under her skirt and she froze.

"Stop," she said.

"Rita—"

"Stop!" She pushed my hand away and withdrew from me. "Jim, I told you—"

"I can't help it,' I said. "I'm only human."

"But I *told* you."

I reached for her again, ready to tell her that I would try to control myself, loving her and hating her and wanting only to hold her close and love her.

Then the door opened.

He was about as tall as I am, but there the similarity ended.

He was built like an ox. His forearms were as thick as my legs and there wasn't an ounce of fat any place on him. It was all hard muscle.

His hair was clipped close to his scalp; his eyes were small and beady. His nose looked as though it had been broken once.

He was wearing clothing that looked familiar. It took me a minute to recognize it.

It was prison clothing.

There was a gun in his right hand that looked like a cannon.

"Out," he said. "Get out of the car." The words came out in a snarl.

I glanced at Rita. She was clutching her blouse around her, trying to button it but having a tough time. Her fingers were numb with fear.

His lips curled into a sneer. "Don't bother," he told her. "I'll just have to rip it off. Now get the hell out of the car."

We got out. There was nothing else to do.

"Over here," he said, motioning with the gun. We walked a few yards from the car into a clearing.

I said, "What do you want?"

He looked at me and smiled. Then he looked at Rita and the smile widened. She stiffened in terror. Her whole body shook.

ONE NIGHT STANDS

"Guess," he said.

I guessed.

"I don't have much money," I said. "But you're welcome to it. And I suppose you'll want the car—it's not new by any means but it'll get you where you're going."

"Yeah," he said. He was still looking at Rita and I knew what he was thinking, what he was going to do.

He turned to me. "Chuck your wallet over here," he said. "And don't try anything. This thing works," he added, motioning with the gun.

I took the wallet from my inside jacket pocket and tossed it to him. He caught it easily with one hand and flipped it open, counting the money.

"Peanuts," he said. "Less than thirty bucks."

"It's all I have."

"With the heap you're driving, that'll hardly cover the gas. And I bet it burns oil by the gallon."

I didn't answer. His eyes went back to Rita and I wished he would stop looking at her, wished he would go away and leave us alone.

"You're nice," he said to her. "It's been a real long time."

She seemed to go limp. I think she probably knew what was happening all along, but as soon as he said those words the full impact of it hit her.

"A long time," he went one. "Too long. You got any idea what it's like."

I looked at him.

"You," he said to me. "You know what it's like being without a woman for four and a half years? Huh?"

I almost started to laugh. I felt like asking him if he knew what it was like being with Rita and not making love to her.

But I didn't say anything.

BRIDE OF VIOLENCE

"Naw," he said. "You wouldn't know. You wouldn't know what it's like sitting in a goddamn cell every night and going crazy. Sitting there forever."

For a second his face seemed to relax. Then it went rigid again and he broke off.

"What did you do?" It was Rita talking this time. I wanted to tell her to shut up, to leave him alone and just pray he would go away without doing what I knew he was going to do. The words stuck in my throat.

"Huh?"

"What did you do that got you in jail?"

He smiled. It wasn't a pretty smile.

"Oh, I did lots of things."

"I mean—"

He walked over to her, keeping the gun trained on me as he did so. Neither of them said anything until he was standing inches away from her. He reached out a finger and chucked her under the chin as if she were a little girl.

"I took something," he said, "something that didn't belong to me."

"What was it?"

He chuckled. "It was a she. A broad. Looked something like you, come to think of it."

She said, "Oh." Her voice was flat and empty, almost lifeless.

"Not quite the same as you," he said. "Wore her hair long but it was a shade darker. Built a lot like you, though."

Without warning his hand snaked out and ripped her blouse all the way open, exposing her breasts. She took a step backward, drawing in her breath sharply as she did so.

He followed her.

"You're not going anywhere," he said. "Understand?"

She nodded dumbly.

ONE NIGHT STANDS

He reached out and fastened a hand on her, and I could see how she shrank from his touch. For a moment I had a wild impulse to charge him. Maybe, with a little luck . . .

But I didn't move. Even if the gun wasn't loaded, even if he didn't manage to shoot me, I still didn't stand a chance. He could take me apart with his bare hands.

His hand tightened on her and she gasped.

"You're built better than she was," he said. "Bigger in the chest anyway. Let's see how your legs stack up against hers."

She didn't move.

"Come on," he said. "Get the skirt off."

It took her a moment to respond. Then she unhooked the skirt and stepped out of it. She wasn't wearing a slip—only a pair of black lace panties that matched the bra which was now in the back seat of the car.

I couldn't help staring at her. Even knowing what was going to happen to her, knowing that we would both be dead in an hour or two at most, I still couldn't help staring at her and realizing how breathtakingly beautiful she was. Her legs were long, with trim ankles and rounded calves leading up to swelling, full thighs.

"Nice," he murmured. "Very nice."

Her mouth opened and closed without any sounds coming out.

"The panties," he said suddenly. "Get 'em off."

"What—"

"Come on," he snapped. "I don't have time to waste."

"What are you going to do to me?"

The smile was back on his face, leering and open and ugly. "You damned little fool," he said. "Now what in hell do you *think* I'm going to do?"

She didn't say anything. I could see the tears welling up in the corners of her eyes.

"I'm going to make up for four and a half years," he said. "Now get the pants off."

"Wait a minute," I said.

BRIDE OF VIOLENCE

He spun toward me and glared at me

"Look," I said, "if you let us go I'll get you more money. I've got a few hundred at home. It'll get you out of the state.

He laughed. "Don't be a damn fool all your life," he said. "We couldn't even make it to your home, and we'd never make the state line. They got the roads blocked off all around."

"They know you escaped?"

"They sure as hell ought to," he said. "I broke out with half the prison watching me."

"But—"

He didn't let me finish. "I haven't got a chance in hell," he said. "By now they've got the whole area sealed off and they'll be closing in soon. They're going to get me."

"Look," I began. "If you let us alone and if you give yourself up maybe they'll go easy on you.

This time his laugh went through me like a cold wind. "Cut the crap," he said. "I was doing life for rape. You think they'll commute my sentence because I gave myself up?"

"But—"

He laughed again, even harsher this time. "I killed a guard on the way out. Shot another one in the gut and he's probably croaked by now. Still think I should give up? Or do you have any more bright ideas?"

I didn't say anything this time.

"I'm just out to get what I can," he said. "Right now I'm going to have some fun with your broad here. Then I'll probably kill the two of you, depending on how I feel. The when the law comes I'll see how many of them I can take with me. And that's all no more time in stir, no more nights in a cell. See?"

I saw.

He turned back to Rita. "The pants," he said. "In a hurry."

She took off her panties, slipping them down over her hips and thighs and stepping out of them. She was shaking like a leaf. It wasn't hard to figure out why.

ONE NIGHT STANDS

"Please," she said suddenly. "Please—don't."

This got him made. "You little bitch," he said. "I'm going to be dead in an hour or two—what the hell is it to you I'd I have some fun first? It's not like I was taking something away from you."

She hesitated. "I . . . I never did it before."

He stared at her. "Huh?"

"I'm a . . . a virgin."

"Sure," he said flatly. "Sure, so am I. We're all virgins. You and him—the two of you were just playing doctor in the back seat. Sure."

"I mean it," she protested. "Jim and I . . . we never went all the way."

He turned to me. "She telling the truth?"

I just nodded.

He looked at her again. Then he looked at me.

Then he started to laugh.

"You little punk," he said when he stopped laughing. "A guy like you, you wouldn't know what to do with a broad like this. What's the bit—just sit around necking?"

My cheeks were burning. But Rita was nodding very earnestly.

"Hell," he said. "I outgrew that when I was in junior high. I guess some people take a while to grow up.

I still don't understand it exactly. When he touched her, when he told me what he was going to do to her, I was still able to stand still and not do anything about it. But now something snapped, as if his insult had hit home and I had to do something about it.

I rushed him.

I came in low and the gun sounded like a cannon when it went off. The shot missed and he pulled the trigger again when I was within a foot or two of him.

The hammer clicked on an empty chamber.

I crashed into him and rolled over on his back. The gun dropped from his hand and I reached for it, managing to pick it up. Then he was on his feet again and coming at me.

BRIDE OF VIOLENCE

Behind me Rita had started to scream.

"You punk," he snarled. "I'll kill you for that."

When he charged me I swung the gun like a club, putting everything I had into it. I had to nail him fast. If he got in one punch he could kill me.

The butt of the gun caught him on the side of the head and knocked him to the ground. It would have killed an ordinary man, or at least knocked him out. But he was shaking his head at once and on his feet a second later.

"Okay," he said. "Now you're going to get it."

I was still holding onto the gun as he came in for the kill. He was wary now, knowing that I had the gun and that I wasn't afraid to hit him with it,

Out of the corner of my eye I could see Rita. She was standing in the same place as before and she was stark naked, screaming her lungs out.

But there was no one around to hear her screams. I cursed myself mentally for parking so far away from town. I had wanted privacy—now I wished I had settled for a nice quiet spot on lover's lane by the river.

It was too late to wish. He stepped in closer, swinging his left like a meat cleaver. When I ducked it he threw the right.

I ducked under the punch and stepped out of the way. He had put his whole body into the blow, expecting it to connect, and now he couldn't stop. He went on right past me and I brought the gun down with all my might on the top of his head.

He dropped like a stone.

I knelt down next to him; he was unconscious. Then everything that had been bottled up inside me let loose and I rolled him onto his back. I brought the butt of the gun down on the bridge of his nose as hard as I could and I heard bone snap.

When somebody who knows judo does that with the side of his hand it can kill a man. I didn't know any more about judo than I had

ONE NIGHT STANDS

read in detective stories, but I wasn't using the side of my hand. I was using a gun-butt.

I felt for a pulse. There was none.

He was dead.

When I straightened up she was in my arms, warm and sobbing and unconscious of her nakedness.

"Jim," she said. "Oh, God!"

I didn't feel anything. "Relax," I said. "He's dead. He can't do anything now."

"You were wonderful," she said. "You . . . you killed him."

I nodded.

"You knocked him out and you killed him."

I nodded again. My arms skipped around her and I stroked he smooth skin.

"He was horrible," she went on. "I . . . never met a man like that."

I mumbled. "He had a few good ideas."

"What did you say?"

I told her again.

She drew away from me. "What do you mean, Jim?"

I ignored her question. Instead I reached out a hand and took hold of her the way he had.

"He's right," I said. "You are nice."

She didn't know how to react. Finally she smiled. "I'm glad you think so."

I didn't smile. I tightened my grip on her the way I had seen him do it and she writhed in pain, staring at me.

"Does it hurt?"

"Yes," she gasped. "What—"

"If you weren't such a bitch," I said, "we wouldn't be here tonight. All this wouldn't have happened."

"I . . . let go, Jim."

I didn't let go.

"Jim—"

54

BRIDE OF VIOLENCE

"We'd have been in bed, Rita. My bed. We never would have seen this guy."

She stared at me. I think she was beginning to catch on.

"Let go," she said. "I have to get dressed."

"Don't bother."

"I have to get some clothes on."

"I'll only rip them off again."

Her eyes opened wider. "Jim—"

"He had some good ideas," I said again. "I'm sick of necking, Rita. When I want something I'm going to take it."

She didn't answer.

"I want you," I said.

"Please," she said. It was the same tone of voice she had used before when he told her to take off her pants.

I managed to laugh. "Lie down," I said. "On the grass. It's not as good as a bed but I'm not going to wait any more. I'm through with waiting, Rita."

She lay down in the grass, trying to cover her nakedness with her hands. Her eyes stared at me dully.

Very methodically I took off my jacket, folded it and set it on the ground by the body. Then I removed the rest of my clothing.

When I knelt beside her she didn't try to resist me but her face was contorted in terror. I put my hand on her shoulder. She shivered.

"Relax," I told here. "It won't be that bad."

I added, "Someday you might even learn to like it."

THE BURNING FURY

He was a big man with a rugged chin and the kind of eyes that could look right through a person, the piercing eyes that said, "I know who you are and I know your angle and I'm not buying it, so get out."

All of him said that—the solid frame without fat on it, the muscles in his arms, and even the way he was dressed. He wore a plaid flannel shirt open at the neck, a pair of tight blue jeans, and heavy logger's boots. Once the boots had been polished to a bright shine, but that was a long time ago. Now they were a dingy brown, scuffed and battered from plenty of hard wear.

He tossed off the shot of rot-gut rye and sipped the beer chaser slowly, wondering how much of the slop he would pour down his gullet tonight. Christ, he was drinking too much. At this rate he'd drink himself broke by the time the season was up and he'd have to go bumming a ride to the next camp. And then it would just start in all over again—breaking your back over the big trees in the daytime and pouring down the rye and beer every night.

The days off were different. On those days it was cheap wine, half-a-buck a bottle Sneaky Pete, down the hatch the first thing in the morning and you kept right on with it until you passed out. That was on your day off, and you needed a day off like you needed a hole in your head.

When he worked he stayed sober until work was through for the day. He didn't need a drink while he was working, not with the full flavor of the open air racing through him and the joy of swinging that double-bit axe and working the big saw, not then. Not when he was up on top, trimming her down and watching the axe bite through branches.

THE BURNING FURY

When he was working there was nothing to forget, no memories to grab him around the neck, no hungers to make him want to reach out and swing at somebody. Not when he had an axe in his hand.

But afterwards, then it was bad. Then the memories came, the Bad Things, and there had to be a way to forget them. The hunger came, stronger each time, and he couldn't sleep unless his gut was filled with whiskey or beer or wine or all three.

If only a man could work twenty-four hours a day...

He knew it would be bad the minute she came through the door. He saw her at once, saw the shape of her body and the color of her hair and the look in her eyes, and he knew right away that it was going to be one hell of a night. He took hold of the beer glass so hard he almost snapped it in two and tossed off the rest of the beer, calling for another shot with his next breath. The bartender came so slowly, and all the time he could see her out of the corner of his eye and feel the hunger come on like a sunset.

It was just like a sunset, the way his mind started going red and yellow and purple all at once and the way the hunger sat there like a big ball of fire nestling on the horizon. He closed his eyes and tried to black out the picture but it stayed with him, glowing and burning and sending hot shivers through his heavy body.

He told the bartender to make it a double, and he threw the double straight down and went to work on the beer chaser, hoping that the boilermakers would work it tonight. Enough liquor would kill the sunset and put out the fire. It worked before. It had to work this time.

He watched her out of the corner of his eye, not wanting to but not able to help himself. She was small—a good head shorter than he was, and she couldn't weigh half of what he did. But the weight she had was all placed just right, just the way he liked a woman to be put together.

Her hair was blonde—soft and fluffy and curling around her face like smoke. Her yellow sweater was just a shade deeper and brighter

ONE NIGHT STANDS

than her hair, and it showed off her body nicely, hugging and emphasizing the gentle curves.

The dark green skirt was tight, and it did things to the other half of her body.

He looked at her, and the ball of fire in his mind burned hotter and brighter every second.

Twenty or twenty-one, he guessed. Young, and with that innocent look that would stay with her no matter what she did or with whom or how often. He knew instinctively that the innocence was an illusion, and he would have known this if he saw her kneeling in a church instead of looking over the men in a logger's bar. But he knew at the same time that this was the only word for what she had: innocence. It was in the eyes, the way she moved, the half-smile on her full lips.

That was what did it: the youth, the innocence, the shape, and the knowledge that she was about as innocent as a Bowery fleabag. That did it every time, those four things all together, and he thought once again that this was going to be one hell of a night.

Another double followed the beer. It was beginning to take hold now, he noticed with a short sigh of relief. He rubbed a calloused finger over his right cheek and noted a sensation of numbness in his cheek, the first sign that the alcohol was reaching him. With his constant drinking it took a little more alcohol every night, but he was getting there now, getting to the point where the girl wouldn't affect him at all.

If only she'd give him time. Just a few more drinks and there would be nothing to worry about, a few more drinks and the numbness would spread slowly from his cheeks to the rest of his body and finally to his brain, quenching the yellow fire and letting him rest.

If only . . .

Out of the corner of his eye, he saw her eyes upon him, singling him out from the crowd at the bar. She took a hesitant step toward him and he wanted to shout "Go away!" at her. She kept on coming,

THE BURNING FURY

and he wished that the stool on his right weren't empty, that with no place for her to sit she might leave him alone.

He finished the chaser and waved again for the bartender. Surely, inevitably, she walked to the bar and took the stool beside him. The dark green skirt caught on the stool and slithered up her leg as she sat, and the sight of firm white flesh heaped fresh fuel upon the mental ball of fire.

He tossed off the shot without tasting it or feeling any effect whatsoever. The beer followed the shot in one swallow, still bringing neither taste nor numbing peace. He winced as she tapped a cigarette twice on the polished surface of the bar and placed it between her lips.

The fumbling in her purse was, he knew, an act and nothing more. Christ, they were all the same, every one of them. He could even time the pitch—it would come on the count of three. One. Two. Thr—

"Do you have a match?"

Right on schedule. He ignored her, concentrating instead on the drink that had appeared magically before him. He hardly remembered ordering it. He couldn't remember anything any more, not since she took the seat beside him, not since every bit of his concentration had been devoted to her.

"A match, please?"

He pulled a box of wooden matches from his shirt pocket without thinking, scratched one on the underside of the bar and held it to her cigarette. She leaned toward him to take the light, moving her leg slightly against his, touching him briefly before withdrawing.

Right on schedule.

He closed the match-box and stuffed it back into his shirt pocket, trying to force his attention back to the drink in front of him. His fingers closed around the shot glass. But he couldn't even seem to lift it from the bar, couldn't raise the drink that might save him for that night at least.

ONE NIGHT STANDS

He wanted to turn to her and snarl: *Look, I'm not interested. I don't care if it's for sale or free for the taking, I'm not interested. Take your hot little body and get the hell out.*

But he didn't even turn around. He sat still, his heavy frame motionless on the stool, waiting for what had to come next.

"You're lonesome aren't you?"

He didn't answer. Christ, even her voice had that sugary innocence, that mixture of sex and baby powder. It was funny he hadn't noticed it before, and he wished he hadn't noticed it now. It just made everything so much worse.

"You're lonesome." It was a statement now, almost a command.

"No, I'm not." Instantly he hated himself for answering at all. The words came from his lips almost by themselves, without him wishing it at all.

"Of course you are. I can tell." She spoke as if she were completely sure of herself, and as she talked her body moved imperceptibly closer to him, her leg inching toward his and pressing against it firmly, not withdrawing this time but remaining there, inflaming him.

His fingers squeezed the shot glass but it stayed on the bar, the rye out of his reach when he needed it so badly.

"Go away." He meant to snap the words at her like axe-blows, but instead they dribbled almost inaudibly from his lips.

"You're lonesome and unhappy. I know."

"Look, I'm fine. Why don't you go bother somebody else?"

She smiled. "You don't mean that," she said. "You don't mean that at all. Besides, I don't want to bother anybody else, can't you see? I want to be with you."

"Why?"

"Because you're big. I like big men."

Sure, he thought. It was like this all the time. "There's other big guys around."

THE BURNING FURY

"Not like you. You got that sad lonesome look, like I can see it a mile away how lonesome you are. And unhappy, you know. It sticks out."

It did; that much was true enough.

"Look," she was saying, "what are you fighting for, huh? You're lonesome and I'm here. You're unhappy and I can make you happy."

When he hesitated, she explained: "I'm good at making guys happy. You'd be surprised."

"I'll bet you are." Christ, why couldn't he just shut up and let her talk herself dry? No, he had to go on making small talk and feeling that hot little leg digging into his and listening to that syrupy voice dripping into his ear like maple syrup into a tin cup. He had to glance at her every second out of the corner of his eye, drinking in the softness of her. His nostrils were filled with the smell of her, a smell that was a mixture of cheap perfume and warm woman-smell, an odor that got into his bloodstream and just made everything worse than ever.

"I can make you happy."

He didn't answer, thinking how happy she would make him if she would just leave now, right away, if the earth would only open up and swallow her or him or both of them, just so long as she would leave him alone. There wasn't much time left.

"Look."

He turned his head involuntarily and watched her wiggle slightly in place, her body moving and rubbing against the sweater and skirt.

"It's all me," she explained. "Under the clothes, I mean."

He clenched his teeth and said nothing.

"I'll make you happy," she said again. When he didn't reply she placed her hand gently on his and repeated the four words in a half-whisper. Her hand was so small, so small and soft.

"C'mon," she said.

He stood up and followed her out the door, the glass of rye still untouched.

ONE NIGHT STANDS

She said her place wasn't far and they walked in the direction she led him, away from the center of town. He didn't say anything all the way, and she only repeated her promise to make him happy. She said it over and over as if it were a magic phrase, a charm of some sort.

His arm went around her automatically and his hand squeezed the firm flesh of her waist. There was no holding back anymore—he knew that, and he didn't try to stop his fingers from gently kneading the flesh or the other hand from reaching for hers and enveloping it possessively. This act served to bring her body right up next to his so that they bumped together with every step. After a block or so her head nestled against his shoulder and remained there for the rest of the walk. The fluffy blonde hair brushed against his cheek.

The cheek wasn't numb anymore.

It was cold out but he didn't notice the cold. It was windy, but he didn't feel the wind cut through the tight blue jeans and the flannel shirt. She had lied slightly: it was a long walk to her place, but he didn't even notice the distance.

She lived by herself in a little shack, a tossed-together affair of unpainted planks with nails knocked in crudely. Somebody had tried to get a garden growing in front but the few plants were all dead now and the weeds over-ran the small patch. He knew, seeing the shack, why she had fixed on the idea of him being lonely. She was so obviously alone, living off by herself and away from the rest of the world.

Inside, she closed and bolted the door and turned to him, her eyes expectant and her mouth waiting to be kissed. He closed his eyes briefly. Maybe he could open them and discover that she wasn't there at all, that he was back at the bar by himself or maybe out cold in his own cabin.

But she was still there when he opened his eyes. She was still standing close to him, her mouth puckered and her eyes vaguely puzzled.

THE BURNING FURY

"I'll make you happy." She said those four words as if they were the answer to every question in the universe, and by this time he thought that perhaps they were.

There was no other answer.

He clenched his teeth again, just as he had done when she squirmed before him on the bar-stool. Then he drove one fist into her stomach and watched her double up in pain, the physical pain of the blow more than matched by the hurt and confusion in her eyes.

He struck her again, a harsh slap on the side of her face that sent her reeling. She started to fall and he brought his knee up, catching her on the jaw and breaking several of her teeth. He hauled her to her feet and the sweater ripped away like tissue paper.

She was right. It was all her underneath.

The next slap started her crying. The one after that knocked the wind out of her and stopped her tears for the time being. His fingers ripped at the skirt and one of his nails dug at her skin, drawing blood. She crumpled to the floor, her whole body shaking with terror and pain, and he fell upon her greedily.

The bitch, he thought. The stupid little bitch.

Couldn't she guess there was only one way to make him happy?

THE DOPE

I'm not very bright. I've never been very smart, and even if I am four years older than Charlie, he's smarter than I am. It's been that way ever since I can remember. When we went to school, I was just one grade ahead of him. He skipped once and I flunked twice, because he's almost as much of a smart guy as I'm a dope. It used to bother the hell out of me, but I got used to it.

Then we both quit after a couple years of high school, and me and Charlie were a team. It was just the two of us. Charlie and Ben, the brains and the brawn. That's the way Charlie used to talk about it. I was lots bigger than him and stronger, but he had a brain like a genius. Let me tell you, we were a team.

Did he have a brain! That's what I used to call him—The Brain. And he used to call me The Muscle, cause I was so strong. Except when I did something stupid he would call me The Dope. He would be kidding when he said it, and he never did it when anyone was around, so I didn't mind too much.

We had it good—just me and Charlie, just the two of us. We didn't stick around at home cause the folks were giving us a hard time ever since we left school. They wanted Charlie to graduate from Erasmus and go to college and be a doctor, but Charlie said the only college he'd ever get to was Sing Sang and he was in no hurry to get there. So we got the hell out of Brooklyn and took a room a ways off Times Square.

Let me tell you, that was the life. We bought some nice clothes, real fancy with sharp colors, and we ate all our meals in restaurants. There were loads of movie houses right around where we lived, and I'd see one or two shows a day. Charlie liked to stay in the room and read. He was a real brain, you see.

And once a week or so we'd pull a job. Charlie did all of the

THE DOPE

planning. He was a clever guy, let me tell you. One day he would go and case a store, and then he wouldn't do anything but plan for the next three or four days. He would sit in the room all by himself and think. He figured every angle.

We went mostly to candy stores. Charlie would get the low-down on how many people worked and what time the store would close, and he figured everything to the minute. Sometimes I wondered why he brought me along. The way he figured things out he could have done it all by himself.

But once in a while he would need me, and that's when I felt real good. Like for instance the time we hit a candy store in Yorkville—that's a German neighborhood uptown on the East Side. There was just this one old guy in the store, like Charlie figured. He was ready to close when we walked in. Charlie bought some candy and talked to the guy and the guy talked back in a thick accent as if he just got off the boat. Then Charlie had enough, and he pulled out his gun and told the guy to empty the cash register. The gun was another of Charlie's ideas. It looked just like a real gun, but all it would shoot was blanks. It's the kind you see advertised in magazines for when burglars come into your house. That way Charlie figured they couldn't pick us up for armed robbery, but we could scare a guy silly by shooting the gun into the air. Now let me ask you how many guys could have figured that out? He was a brain.

But to get back to the story, the old guy gave us a hard time. He started rattling off a mile a minute in German and he got real loud. So Charlie just turned to me and said, "Take him, Muscle."

That's all he had to say, and he said it just like that. That was what I was waiting for. I stepped right in and belted the guy one in the mush, but not too hard. He went out like a light, let me tell you. We emptied the cash box and got the hell out quick.

Those were the days. I was happy, you know. I didn't talk, much, but I tried to tell Charlie how happy I was. Most of the time he just nodded, but one time he got mad.

"Happy?" he said. "What the hell are you happy about? We're

ONE NIGHT STANDS

a couple of small-time mugs living in a dump. What's to be happy?"

I tried to tell him how nice it was, going to shows and just the two of us living together, but I don't talk too good.

"You Dope," he said. "You'd be happy being a punk forever. That's not for me, Dope."

I couldn't see what he was getting at so I went out to a show. It was this picture where Jimmy Cagney wants to be the top man in the rackets so his mother will be proud of him and he winds up getting blown up in a factory. It was a damn good picture, except for the ending.

When I got back to the room Charlie was sitting on the bed writing something down. I got excited, cause I knew he was making notes for the next job. He always wrote everything out in detail, and burned his notes in the wastebasket. He didn't miss a trick.

I sat down next to him and gave him a smile. "What's new, Brain?" He didn't answer until he finished what he was writing, and then he smiled back at me. "A big one," he said. "No more candy store junk."

I didn't answer and he went on to explain it. I didn't get it all because I'm not too bright when it comes to that kind of thing, but there was some sort of office he knew about where they had the payroll set up at night and if we went in and robbed it we could get away with the whole payroll. He asked me didn't it beat knocking over candy stores and I told him it sure did. I guy like me never would have figured out something like that, but Charlie was sharp as a tack.

We pulled the job the next night. It was just a few blocks away from where we lived, and the place was all locked up. Charlie said there was a watchman on duty in the back, where the money was. Then he took a little hunk of metal and got the door open. I don't know where he learned how to do that, I really don't.

I started to walk right in but Charlie made me slow down. He whispered that the old guy could give an alarm unless we got him by surprise. We walked in on tiptoe, and we were practically on top of

THE DOPE

him before he looked up, and Charlie had the fake gun pointed right at him. I thought he'd have a heart attack then and there.

"Open the safe," Charlie said.

The old guy just stared for a minute, and then he stuck out his chin. "You boys better go home," he said. "I'll give you ten seconds before I call the cops."

Charlie knew how to put the screws on. He didn't say a word, but just kept standing there with the gun pointing right at the guy's head. It was so real that I almost started thinking it wasn't a phony gun with blank bullets.

Then the guy jumped. He fell right down off the chair, and Charlie yelled, "Get him, you goddamn dope!"

I went for him then, but he hit the alarm button before I could get him and the bells started ringing like mad. I was boiling then. I yanked him up off the floor and belted him all the way across the room, and his head hit the wall like Ted Williams hits a baseball.

I started across the room after him, I was so mad. But Charlie stopped me and we ran out. There were people all around, but they didn't know what was happening and we managed to get back to the room.

Charlie wouldn't even talk to me. He sat on the bed listening to the radio, and when the news came that the guy had died of a broken skull he looked at me like I was the stupidest guy in the world. Let me tell you, I felt horrible. It was just like me to swing too hard.

I thought we could still get away, but Charlie straightened me out. He told me how they saw us and they'd get us sooner or later. And he figured out the only way we could get out of it.

We wiped off his gun and got my fingerprints on it, and then we went to the police station. I told them the story just like Charlie told me to, about how I was the older brother and I was bigger than Charlie and made him come along and commit crimes, and how I beat up the guy and killed him. And then at the trial some doctor told how I was a dope and hardly knew what I was doing, and they shouldn't blame me for it. Charlie had to go to jail, but he got out in a year.

ONE NIGHT STANDS

Because I was such a dope they only gave me ten years for manslaughter.

It's not bad here, either. There are lots of nice guys to talk to, and the food's okay. And the best part of it is that Charlie's out now, and he comes to visit me once a month. He sends me money for cigarettes and everything, which is damn nice of him.

I'm just a dope, but I'm lucky. Most guys wouldn't pay any attention to me, especially if they were real smart. But Charlie comes every month, and he says, "Hi, Muscle," and I say, "Hiya, Brain."

We're still buddies, even after what I did.

He's a wonderful brother, let me tell you.

A FIRE AT NIGHT

He gazed silently into the flame. The old tenement was burning, and the smoke was rising upward to merge against the blackness of the sky. There were neither stars nor moon in the sky, and the street lights in the neighborhood were dim and spaced far apart. Nothing detracted from the brilliance of the fire. It stood out against the night like a diamond in a pot of bubbling tar. It was a beautiful fire.

He looked around and smiled. The crowd was growing larger, as everyone in the area thronged together to watch the building burn. They like it, he thought. Everyone likes a fire. They receive pleasure from staring into the flames, watching them dance on the tenement roof. But their pleasure could never match his, for it was his fire. It was the most beautiful fire he had ever set.

His mind filled with the memory of it. It had been planned to perfection. When the sun dropped behind the tall buildings and the sky grew dark, he had placed the can of kerosene in his car with the rags—plain, non-descript rags that could never be traced to him. And then he had driven to the old tenement. The lock on the cellar door was no problem, and there was no one around to get in the way. The rags were placed, the kerosene was spread, the match was struck, and he was on his way. In seconds the flames were licking at the ancient walls and racing up the staircases.

The fire had come a long way now. It looked as though the building had a good chance of caving in before the blaze was extinguished. He hoped vaguely that the building would fall. He wanted his fire to win.

He glanced around again, and was amazed at the size of the crowd. All of them pressed close, watching his fire. He wanted to call to them. He wanted to scream out that it was his fire, that he and he alone had created it. With effort he held himself back. If he cried

ONE NIGHT STANDS

out it would be the end of it. They would take him away and he would never set another fire.

Two of the firemen scurried to the tenement with a ladder. He squinted at them, and recognized them—Joe Dakin and Roger Haig. He wanted to call hello to them, but they were too far away to hear him. He didn't know them well, but he felt as though he did. He saw them quite often.

He watched Joe and Roger set the ladder against the side of the building. Perhaps there was someone trapped inside. He remembered the other time when a small boy had failed to leave the building in time. He could still hear the screams — loud at first, then softer until they died out to silence. But this time he thought the building had been empty.

The fire was beautiful! It was warm and soft as a woman. It sang with life and roared with joy. It seemed almost a person, with a mind and a will of its own.

Joe Dakin started up the ladder. Then there must be someone in the building. Someone had not left in time and was trapped with the fire. That was a shame. If only there were a way for him to warn them! Perhaps next time he could give them a telephone call as soon as the blaze was set.

Of course, there was even a beauty in trapping someone in the building. A human sacrifice to the fire, an offering to the goddess of Beauty. The pain, the loss of life was unfortunate, but the beauty was compensation. He wondered who might be caught inside.

Joe Dakin was almost to the top of the ladder. He stopped at a window on the fifth floor and looked inside. The he climbed through.

Joe is brave, he thought. I hope he isn't hurt. I hope he saves the person in the building.

He turned around. There was a little man next to him, a little man in shabby clothes with a sad expression on his face. He reached over and tapped the man on the shoulder.

"Hey!" he said. "You know who's in the building?"

The little man nodded wordlessly.

A FIRE AT NIGHT

"Who is it?"

"Mrs. Pelton," said the little man. "Morris Pelton's mother."

He had never heard of Morris Pelton. "Well, Joe'll get her out. Joe's a good fireman."

The little man shook his head. "Can't get her out," he said. "Can't nobody get her out."

He felt irritated. Who was this little jerk to tell him? "What do you mean?" he said. "I tell you Joe's a helluva fireman. He'll take care of it."

The little man flashed him a superior look. "She's fat," he said. "She's a real big woman. She must weigh two hundred pounds easy. This Joe's just a little guy. How's he gonna get her out? Huh?" The little man tossed his head triumphantly and turned away without an answer.

Another sacrifice, he thought. Joe would be disappointed. He'd want to rescue the woman, but she would die in the fire.

He looked at the window. Joe should come out soon. He couldn't save Mrs. Pelton, and in a few seconds he would be coming down the ladder. And then the fire would burn and burn and burn, until the walls of the building crumbled and caved in, and the fire won the battle. The smoke would curl in ribbons from the ashes. It would be wonderful to watch.

He looked up at the window suddenly. Something was wrong. Joe was there at last, but he had the woman with him. Was he out of his mind?

The little man had not exaggerated. The woman was big, much larger than Joe. He could barely see Joe behind her, holding her in his arms. Joe couldn't sling her into a fireman's carry; she would have broken his back.

He shuddered. Joe was going to try to carry her down the ladder, to cheat the fire of its victim. He held her as far from his body as he could and reached out a foot gingerly. His foot found the first rung and rested on it.

ONE NIGHT STANDS

He took his other foot from the windowsill and reached out for the next rung. He held tightly to the woman, who was screaming now. Her body shook with each scream, and rolls of fat bounced up and down.

The damned fool, he thought. How could he expect to haul a fat slob like that down five flights on a ladder? He was a good fireman, but he didn't have to act like a superman. And the fat bitch didn't even know what was going on. She just kept screaming her head off. Joe was risking his neck for her, and she didn't even appreciate it at all.

He looked at Joe's face as the fireman took another halting step. Joe didn't look good. He had been inside the building too long. The smoke was bothering him.

Joe took another step and tottered on the ladder. Drop her, he thought. You goddamned fool, let go of her!

And then he did. The woman slipped suddenly from Joe's grip, and plummeted downward to the sidewalk. Her scream rose higher and higher as she fell, and then stopped completely. She struck the pavement like a bug smacking against the windshield of a car.

His whole being filled with relief. Thank God, he thought. It was too bad for the woman, but now Joe would reach the ground safely. But he noticed that Joe seemed to be in trouble. He was still swaying back and forth. He was coughing, too.

And then, all at once, Joe fell. He left the ladder and began to drop to the earth. His body hovered in the air and floated down like a feather. Then he hit the ground and melted into the pavement.

At first he could not believe it. Then he glared at the fire. Damn you, he thought. You weren't satisfied with the old woman. You had to take a fireman too.

It wasn't right.

The fire was evil. This time it had gone too far. Now it would have to suffer for it.

And then he raised his hose and trained it on the burning hulk of the tenement, punishing the fire.

FROZEN STIFF

At ten minutes to five the Mexican kid finished sweeping the floor. He stood by the counter, leaning on his broom and looking at the big white-faced clock.

"Go on home," Brad told him. "Nobody's going to want any lamb chops delivered anymore. You're through, go get some rest."

The kid flashed teeth in a smile. He took off his apron and hung it on a peg, put on a poplin windbreaker.

"Take it easy," Brad said.

"You stayin' here?"

"For a few minutes," Brad said. "I got a few things to see to."

The kid walked to the door, then turned at the last moment. "You watch out for the freezer, Mr. Malden. You get in there, man, nobody can get you out."

"I'll be careful."

"I'll see you Mr. Malden."

"Yeah," Brad said. "Sure."

The kid walked out. Brad watched the door close after him, then walked behind the meat counter and leaned over it, his weight propped up on his elbows. He was a big man, heavy with muscle, broad-faced and barrel-chested. He was forty-six, and he looked years younger until you saw the furrowed forehead and the drawn, anxious lines at the corners of his mouth. Then he looked fifty.

He took a deep breath and let it out slowly. He picked a heavy cleaver from a hook behind him, lifted it high overhead and brought it down upon a wooden chopping block. The blade sank four inches into the block.

Strong, he thought. Like an ox.

He left the cleaver in the block. The freezer was in the back, and he walked through a sawdust-covered hallway to it. He opened the

ONE NIGHT STANDS

door and looked inside. Slabs of beef hung from the ceiling. Other cuts and sections of meat were piled on the floor. There were cleavers and hooks on pegs in the walls. The room was very cold.

He looked at the inside of the door. There was a safety latch there, installed so that the door could be opened from the inside if a person managed to lock himself in.

Two days ago he had smashed the safety latch. He broke it neatly and deliberately with a single blow of the cleaver, and then he told the Mexican kid what had happened.

"Watch yourself in the cold bin," he had told the kid. "I busted the goddam latch. That door shuts on you and you're in trouble. The room's soundproof. Nobody can hear you if you yell. So make damn sure the door's open when you're in there."

He told Vicki about it that same night. "I did a real smart thing today," he said. "Broke the damn safety latch on the cold bin door."

"So what?" she said.

"So I got to watch it," he said. "The door shuts when I'm in there and there's no way out. A guy could freeze to death."

"You should have it fixed."

"Well," he had said, shrugging, "one of these days."

He stood looking into the cold bin for a few more moments now. Then he turned slowly and walked back to the front of the store. He closed the door, latched it. He turned off the lights. Then he went back to the cold bin.

He opened the door. This time he walked inside, stopping the door with a small wooden wedge. The wedge left the door open an inch or so. He took a deep breath, filling his lungs with icy air.

He looked at his watch. Five-fifteen, it read. He took another breath and smiled slowly, gently, to himself.

By eight or nine he would be dead.

It started with a little pain in the chest. Just a twinge, really. It hurt him when he took a deep breath, and sometimes it made him cough. A little pain—you get to expect them now and then when you

FROZEN STIFF

pass forty. The body starts to go to hell in one way or the other and you get a little pain from time to time.

He didn't go to the doctor. What the hell, a big guy like Brad Malden, he should go to the doctor like a kid every time he gets a little pain? He didn't go to the doctor. Then the pain got worse, and he started getting other pains in his stomach and legs, and he had a six-letter idea what it was all about.

He was right. By the time he went to a doctor, finally, it was inoperable. "You should have come in earlier," the doctor told him. "Cancer's curable, you know. We could have taken out a lung—"

Sure, he thought. And I could breath with my liver. Sure.

"I want to get you to the hospital right away," the doctor had said.

And he asked, reasonably, "What the hell for?"

"Radium treatments. Radical surgery. We can help you, make the pain easier, delay the progress of the disease—"

Make me live longer, he had thought. Make it last longer, and hurt longer, and cost more.

"Forget it," he said.

"Mr. Malden—"

"Forget it. Forget I came to you, understand? I never came here, I never saw you, period. Got it?"

The doctor did not like it that way. Brad didn't care whether he liked it or not. He didn't have to like it. It wasn't his life.

He took a deep breath again and the pain was like a knife in his chest. Like a cleaver. Not for me, he thought. No lying in bed for a year dying by inches. No wasting away from two hundred pounds to eighty pounds. No pain. No dribbling away the money on doctors and hospitals until he was gone and there was nothing left for Vicki but a pile of bills that the insurance would barely cover. Thanks, doc. But no thanks. Not for me.

He looked again at his watch. Five-twenty. Go ahead, he told himself angrily. Get rid of the wedge, shut the door, lie down and go to sleep. It was cold, and you closed your eyes and relaxed, and bit by bit you got numb all over. Go ahead, shut the door and die.

ONE NIGHT STANDS

But he left the wedge where it was. No rush, he thought. There was plenty of time for dying.

He walked to the wall, leaned against it. This was the better way. In the morning they would find him frozen to death, and they would figure logically enough that the wedge had slipped and he had frozen to death. Vicki would cry over him and bury him, and the insurance policy would pay her a hundred thousand dollars. He had fifty thousand dollars of straight life insurance with a double indemnity clause for accidental death, and this could only be interpreted as an accident. With that kind of money Vicki could get a decent income for life. She was young and pretty, they didn't have any kids, in a few years she could remarry and start new.

Fine.

The pain came, and this time it was sharp. He doubled over, clutching at his chest. God, he hoped the doctor would keep his mouth shut. Though it would still go as accidental death. It had to. No one committed suicide by locking himself in a cold bin. They jumped out of windows, they slashed their wrists, they took poison, they left the gas jets on. They didn't freeze themselves like a leg of lamb. Even if they suspected suicide, they had to pay the claim. They were stuck with it.

When the next stab of pain came he couldn't stand any longer. It had been hell trying not to wince, trying to conceal the pain from Vicki. Now he was alone; he didn't have to hide it. He hugged both hands to his chest and sank slowly to the floor. He sat on a slab of bacon, then moved the slab aside and sat on the floor. The floor was very cold. Hell, he thought, it was funny to sit in the cold bin. He'd never spent much time there before, just walked in to get some meat or to hang some up. It was a funny feeling, sitting on the floor.

How cold was it? He wasn't sure exactly. The thermostat was outside by the door; otherwise the suicide wouldn't have been possible, since he could have turned up the temperature. The damn place was a natural, he thought. A death trap.

FROZEN STIFF

He put his hand to his forehead. Getting cold already, he thought. It shouldn't take too long, not at this rate. And he didn't even have the door closed. He should close the door now. It would go a little faster with the door closed.

Could he smoke a cigarette? Sure, he thought. Why not?

He considered it. If they found the cigarette they would know he'd had a smoke before he froze to death. So? Even if it were an accident, a guy would smoke, wouldn't he? Besides, he'd make damn sure they'd think he tried to get out. Flail at the door with the cleaver, throw some meat around, things like that. They wouldn't make a federal case out of a goddam cigarette.

He took one out, put it between his lips, scratched a match and lighted it. He smoked thoughtfully, wincing slightly when the pain gripped his chest like a vise. A year of this? No, not for him. The quick death was better.

Better for him. Better for Vicki, too. God, he loved that woman! Too much, maybe. Sometimes he got the feeling that he loved her too hard, that he cared more for her than she did for him. Well, it was only natural. He was a fatheaded butcher, not too bright, not much to look at. She was twenty-six and beautiful and there were times when he couldn't understand why she had married him in the first place. Couldn't understand, but remained eternally grateful.

The cigarette warmed his fingers slightly. They were growing cold now, and their tips were becoming numb. All he had to do was flip the wedge out. It wouldn't take long.

He finished the cigarette, put it out. He was on his way to get rid of the wedge when he heard the front door open.

It could only be Vicki, he thought. No one else had a key. He heard her footsteps, and he smiled quickly to himself. Then he heard her voice and he frowned.

"He must be here," she was saying. Her voice was a whisper. "In the back."

"Let's go."

ONE NIGHT STANDS

A man's voice, that one. He walked to the cold bin door and put his face to the one-inch opening. When they came into view he stiffened. She was with a man, a young man. He had a gun in one hand. She went into his arms and he kissed her hard.

Vicki, he thought! God!

They were coming back now. He moved away, moved back into the cold bin, waiting. The door opened and the man was pointing a gun at him and he shivered. The pain came, like a sword, and he was shaking. Vicki mistook it for fear and grinned at him.

She said, "Wait, Jay."

The gun was still pointing at him. Vicki had her hand on the man's arm. She was smiling. Evil, Brad thought. Evil.

"Don't shoot him," she was saying. "It was a lousy idea anyway. Killed in a robbery—who the hell robs a butcher shop? You know how much dough he takes in during a day? Next to nothing."

"You got a better way, Vicki?"

"Yes," she said. "A much better way."

And she was pulling Jay back, leading him away from the door. And then she was kicking the wooden wedge aside, and laughing, and shutting the door. He heard her laughter, and he heard the terribly final sound the door made when it clicked shut, and then he did not hear anything at all. They were leaving the shop, undoubtedly making all sorts of sounds. The cold bin was soundproof. He heard nothing.

He took a deep, deep breath, and the pain in his chest knocked him to his knees.

You should have waited, he thought. One more minute, Vicki, and I could have done it myself. Your hands would be clean, Vicki. I could have died happy, Vicki. I could have died not knowing.

You're a bitch, Vicki.

Now lie down, he told himself. Now go to sleep, just the way you planned it yourself. Nothing's different. And you can't get out, because you planned it this way. You're through.

78

FROZEN STIFF

Double indemnity. The bitch was going to collect double indemnity!

No, he thought. No.

It took him fifteen minutes to think of it. He had to find a way, and it wasn't easy. If they thought about murder they would have her, of course. She'd left prints all over the cold-bin door. But they would not be looking for prints, not the way things stood. They'd call it an accident and that would be that. Which was the trouble with setting things up so perfectly.

He could make it look like suicide. That might cheat her out of the insurance. He could slash his wrists or something, or —

No.

He could cheat her out of more than the insurance.

It took awhile, but he worked it out neatly. First he scooped up his cigarette butt and stuck it in his pants pocket. Then he scattered the ashes around. Step one.

Next he walked to the rear of the cold bin and took a meat cleaver from the peg on the wall. He set the cleaver on top of a hanging side of beef, gave the meat a push. The cleaver toppled over and plummeted to the floor. It landed on the handle and bounced.

He tried again with another slab of meat. He tried time after time, until he found the piece that was just the right distance from the floor and found just the spot to set the cleaver. When he nudged the meat, the cleaver came down, turned over once, and landed blade-down in the floor.

He tried it four times to make sure it would work. It never missed. Then he picked the cleaver from the floor, wiped his prints from the blade and handle with his apron, and placed the cleaver in position on top of the hunk of meat. It was a leg of lamb, the meat blood-red, the fat sickly white. He sat down on the floor, then stretched out on his back looking up at the leg of lamb. Good meat, he thought. Prime.

ONE NIGHT STANDS

He smiled, tensed with pain from his chest and stomach, relaxed and smiled again. Not quite like going to sleep this way, he thought. Not painless, like freezing. But faster.

He lifted a leg, touched his foot to the leg of lamb. He gave it a gentle little push, and the cleaver sliced through the air and found his throat.

HATE GOES COURTING

I should have figured it the second day. By that time you have to see it unless you shut your eyes, and if you shut your eyes you just about deserve what happens.

It was the wind. It's that wind you get out on a plain or desert and almost nowhere else, the kind of wind that builds up miles away and comes at you and keeps on going right through you and on into the next county. Clothes don't help. If you're in the desert the sand goes right through your clothes, and if you put a wet handkerchief over your face the wind blows the sand right through the handkerchief.

When you're up north you freeze. The wind ices you right through.

And when you're in Kansas there's just the wind coming at you like a sword through a piece of silk, just the wind and nothing else. It's a sweeping wind, not the twister that blew Dorothy to Oz and knocks over a house now and then. The sky clouds up and the sun disappears and the damned wind is all over the place. Then it rains water by the pound and when it clears up the air is still and quiet.

That's how it usually happens, and that's why I couldn't have figured it out on the first day, not even with my eyes wide open. But the second day I should have known. On the second day there was still no rain, no storm at all, and the wind was blowing all over and harder than before.

It happens that way once in a while. It happens, with the wind holding up forever like it's never going to stop, and in Kansas they call it the bad wind. It blows forever, and it blows your tendons so tight you think they're going to snap on you.

And something happens. Something like a man dying or a house burning, something bad.

That's why I should have known—if I had my eyes open.

ONE NIGHT STANDS

The afternoon of the second day we were out hunting jacks in the north field. The wind was coming from the west, bending the long grasses all the way over and holding them there. We were hunting into the wind; it didn't make too much sense that way, but it was late and we were headed back home, and back home meant walking into the wind.

"Bet she's been here," Brad was saying. "Not hunting—"

Lady let out a burst of good baying, sounding the way a good beagle sounds, and she cut off the rest of his sentence.

"You hear me, John?"

I nodded at him but he wasn't looking at me. He was about twenty yards ahead of me and it was no use talking into the wind. It just shoves the words right back into your mouth. You can shout at it, but I didn't much feel like shouting. I didn't feel like answering, when you come right down to it.

"You hear me? She's been out here plenty of times."

My cap was down over my ears but I could still hear him good and clear. We could have gone home right then. The bag was full of jacks, nice husky ones that Lady ran down like a champion, more rabbit than we could eat in the next year and a half. But going home wouldn't do any good. Brad was a tough guy to shut up.

"Nice soft grass out here. Her nice little body would fit real cozy in it, you know?"

I looked down at the grass without meaning to and my head started to ache.

"Know what we used to call a woman like that? Called them 'sweethearts of the fleet.' There's lots like her, Brother John. She's not the only little tramp in the—"

"Shut up."

"World. But you wouldn't know, would you? Old John stays on the farm through thick and thin. Doesn't let the glitter of the outside world knock his life apart. Sober Old John. You ever fixing to see the world, brother?"

"Maybe."

HATE GOES COURTING

"Sure. I hear you went to Omaha once. Like it?"

"It was all right." I didn't want to answer him. I never wanted to answer him, but that didn't make much difference. It was always like that—him needling and pushing and prodding and me taking it and answering when I was supposed to.

When he was in the Navy it was nice. Pa and I made the farm run, coming out ahead in a good year and squeezing by in a bad one. Hunting with Lady and catching a movie in town now and then, and a long sleep at night and good food and plenty of it.

But with Brad around you don't sleep much. Ma died giving birth to him, and he's been killing the rest of us since then. Brad was a smart little brother, a real sharp little fellow.

Brad and I never got along.

"You like Omaha, huh? That's good—glad to hear it. But how does it stack up next to all the other big towns?"

This time I didn't answer.

"Did you really do the town or just go to the feed store? I hear they have a real fine feed store in Omaha. Lots of feed and all."

"Stop it."

He said something that I didn't catch, and then he said a little louder, "How does Margie stack up next to the Omaha chippies?"

I wanted to kill him. If he were right close instead of twenty yards off, I would have hit him. I could feel the bag slipping off my shoulder and my fist balling up and sinking into that soft belly of his. My fist would have gone through him like the wind was going through me right then.

I should have raised the gun and shot his head off.

Instead I clenched one fist and let it relax. I didn't say anything.

"She'd make a good one," he said. "It's her trade, all right. She's got the shape for it. And plenty long years of experience."

"Stop it, Brad."

"All she'd have to do," he went on, "is what they call relinquishing her amateur standing. Just sell it instead of giving it

ONE NIGHT STANDS

away. But maybe she likes it too much to set a price on it. Is it as good as I hear it is?"

"You never touched her."

It was out of me before I could stop it. It was part question even though I knew he hadn't. I had to make sure and I had to tell myself, and at the same time I didn't want to know if he had. It didn't matter. It didn't make any difference at all, but I just didn't want to hear about it.

"You sure about that Brother John? Well, maybe yes and maybe no. But I guess I'm fixing to try her, all right. If she's as good as everybody says, I must be missing a hell of a lot. Is she that good?"

I closed my eyes and listened to the wind. His voice seemed to come over the wind, cutting and burning just like that wind, just as bad and holding up just as long.

"Or are you waiting until you're married? Is that it, Brother John? That's a good one—waiting it out on the town tramp!"

He started to laugh. His laugh was like the wind, ice cold and mean as a mad dog, cutting like a sword through a piece of silk. I gave a whistle for Lady and she came like she always did and I headed back toward home, walking away and leaving him laughing that laugh of his in the middle of the fields.

Ten minutes later I was still walking and I could still hear him laughing and the wind was as bad as ever.

He didn't understand.

Nobody understood the whole thing, but no one else got on my back the way Brad did. Everybody knew about Margie, but everybody else kept to their own business and let me mind my own.

Except for Brad.

The others knew about Margie, but they also knew that Margie was different, that she wasn't like any other woman who ever lived. It was something they could feel even if they didn't know just why.

She was beautiful. That was something all of them could see. It wasn't exactly hard to see; it jumped out at you until all you were conscious of was the beauty of her. Her hair was the color of corn

HATE GOES COURTING

and she wore it long, letting it flow down pure and golden and glowing. Her body was so smooth and rounded that she seemed to be made out of liquid. She looked like she was moving even when she was standing absolutely still.

When she slept, she looked like a big cat crouched and ready to spring.

Her skin was clear as a cameo. Her mouth was tiny and red and her eyes were a soft brown and her ears were little shells covered with a furry fuzz.

These were things that anybody could see—even Brad.

But nobody else could see inside. Nobody else could see her eyes when she cried because she never cried when anybody else was around. Most of her beauty was inside, and nobody else could see inside her. Their eyes stopped at the clear skin and the corn-colored hair and the gently curved body, and that is why I was the only person who ever knew Margie.

The others never knew how she felt in your arms when she was very happy or very sad. I don't give a damn how many arms she's been in; she's only happy or sad with me. With the others she crawled into a shell as thin and tight as skin, and the others think that shell is Margie.

But it isn't.

I felt sorry for the others, if you want to know the truth. I felt sorry for them because they never stayed all night with Margie and woke up with her tears matting the hair on their chests and her body warm and quiet.

When I asked her to marry me she cried more than ever and told me I was crazy and I didn't mean it. Then she said, yes, and cried some more and we made love so beautifully that even thinking about it weeks later made me shake a little.

I finished cleaning the gun and set it up on the rack on the wall. I skinned the rabbits and dressed them and salted them down, and then I washed up and changed my shirt and headed towards Margie's

ONE NIGHT STANDS

place. She lived by herself in a little cabin on the outskirts of the town.

Days she clerked in the five-and-dime in town, but that was going to change. She'd be coming to my place and she'd be my woman, and then she wouldn't have to work any more. She didn't have to do a thing she didn't want to. She could just lie around the house all day loving me.

That would be enough.

The moon was up by the time I got to her cabin. The moon was round and bright and golden and it floated like a California orange. When I opened Margie's door, the wind nearly tore it clear off its hinges.

The wind blew all night long, but I didn't hear it.

I think the wind set a record for our part of Kansas. It kept up day after day, each day a little worse than the last, and you could tell there was more than a storm brewing. You could smell it the way the wheat was bowed over so much it looked like it grew that way.

The wind was all over. There was a rush of accidents—a two-car head-on collision at the intersection of Mill Run and 68, a blow-out just a mile from our house, a freak accident with a telephone pole dropping on a parked car.

Nobody walked away from those accidents. Five people died in the two-car deal and a salesman got sandwiched in the blow-out when his car turned over. And there were two kids from the high school in the back seat of that parked car. You couldn't tell which was which, the way the telephone pole pressed their bodies together.

It sounded silly, but everybody knew it was the wind. And the wind kept blowing without a storm.

And the wind was in Brad, the way he kept up with his needling and prodding. He was getting through to me more often and my hand was sore from making a fist and relaxing it. He made up stories about Margie and who she went with and what they did and how many times and other crazy things. I just couldn't take it anymore.

HATE GOES COURTING

"I'm telling you this for your own good," he would say. "Hell—get what you can. I don't blame you for that. But I have to keep you from marrying her. I've gotta look out for my older brother. You farmers don't know all the angles."

That got Pa mad. He started off how there was nothing wrong with being a farmer and how it wasn't as bad as the Navy where all you did was ride a tin boat or maybe kill some folk if there was a war on.

Every day was just that much worse than the last.

But when it happened I wasn't ready for it. I walked to her place in a harder and colder wind than ever, and when I got there she was all alone. She was sitting hunched up on her bed with her head almost touching her knees and her hair falling down over her face. I couldn't see her face. I pulled the door shut and walked over to her.

When I went to give her a kiss she turned her face to the wall and wouldn't look at me. I knew something was wrong, and I guess I knew just what it was, but I was hoping so hard that I wouldn't let myself believe it.

I sat down on the bed next to her and pulled her over to me. She didn't pull away. I let her head rest in my lap and ran my fingers through that long silky hair. I thought I could get her to cry it out but she wouldn't cry, not a single tear. Her whole body was shaking with something but she wouldn't open up and let it out. I just sat there stroking her hair and not saying a thing.

Then she looked at me and she started to cry. She cried for a long time, crying all the sickness and sadness out of her, when it was done she was better and I knew she would be all right.

It wouldn't leave a scar.

It was done.

The walk home was a long one even with the wind behind me. He was waiting for me, and when I came in he looked at me and he knew that I knew.

He said, "She was nice, Brother John. But I've had better."

ONE NIGHT STANDS

I just looked at him. I didn't bother to tell him that he never had her, that I was the only man to have her, ever.

He wouldn't have known what I was talking about.

"You ought to get around more," he said. "Oughta see what the rest of the world's like. You know?"

The vein in my temple started throbbing just the way Margie's did before.

"There's other women. Bet you'll find some that's even better in the sack than she is, Brother John."

When you're up close a shotgun makes a big messy hole, big as a man's fist, but when I squeezed that trigger the shell went through him like a sword through a piece of silk, like the wind blowing outside. He let out a moan and put both hands over the hole in his stomach and sat down slowly. His eyes were staring like he couldn't believe it happened.

His eyes got glassy, but they stayed open that way, staring at me.

Outside the wind broke and it started to rain.

Fifteen months and I'll be out. The law's the law, but the people around here know me and they knew Brad, and the law can bend a little when it has to.

Margie will be waiting for me. I know she will.

I DON'T FOOL AROUND

Fischer pulled up at a curb and we got out of the car in a hurry, heading for the black Chevy with the people standing around it. The precinct cop made room for us and we went on through. As far as I was concerned, this was just a formality. I knew who was dead and I knew who had killed him. Taking a good long look at the corpse wasn't going to change that.

The punk slumped over the wheel with holes in his head had lived longer than we had expected. He was a hood named Johnny Blue, a strongarm-weakbrain who crossed some of the wrong people. He'd been due for a hit for weeks, according to the rumbles that filtered through to Manhattan West. Now he'd been hit, and hard.

One slug in the side of the face. Another in the neck. Three more in the back of the head.

"Who is he?" Fischer asked. I told him.

"A messy way to do it," the kid went on. "Any of those shots would have killed him. Why shoot him up like that?"

My college cop. My new partner, my cross to bear ever since some genius switched Danny Taggert to Vice. My Little Boy Lost, who wanted murder to be a nice clean affair, with one bullet lodged in the heart and, if you please, as little blood as possible.

I said, "The killer didn't want to take chances."

"Chances? But—"

I was very tired. "This wasn't a tavern brawl," I told him. "This wasn't one guy hitting another guy over the head with a bar stool. This was a pro killing."

"It doesn't look so professional to me. A mess."

"That's because you don't know what to look for." I turned away, sick of the corpse and the killer, sick of Fischer, sick of the West 46th Street at three in the morning. Sick of murder.

ONE NIGHT STANDS

"It's a pro killing," I said again. "In a car, on a quiet street, in the middle of the night. Five bullets, any one of which would have caused death. That's a trademark."

"Why?"

"Because hired killers don't fool around," I said. "Let's get out of here."

The coffee was bitter but it was black and it was hot. I sipped it as I read through the file again. I knew everything in the file by heart. I read it automatically, then shoved it over to Fischer.

"Name," I said, "Frank Calder. First arrest at age 14, 1948, grand theft auto. Suspended. Arrested three months later, GTA again, six months in Elmira. Three years later he was picked up for assault with a deadly weapon. A knife. The victim refused to press charges and we dropped them."

I sipped some more of the coffee. "That was eight years ago. Since then he's been picked up fifteen times. Same charge each time. Suspicion of homicide."

"Innocent?"

"Guilty, of course. Fifteen times that we know about. Probably a dozen more that we don't know about. Fourteen times we let him go. Once we thought we had a case."

"What happened?"

"Grand jury disagreed with us. Indictment quashed."

Fischer nodded. "And you think he may have killed Blue?"

"No."

"Then why are we—"

"I don't *think* he *might* have killed Blue," I said. "I know damn well he killed Blue. Calder does most of his work in the Kitchen. A Hell's Kitchen boy from the start, grew up on 39th Street west of Ninth. Gun used was a .38. Calder always uses a .38. Likes to shoot people in cars."

"Still, you can't be sure that—"

"I can be sure," I cut in. I wished that Vice would send Danny back to me. Fischer was impossible. "Calder works for Nino Popo

I DON'T FOOL AROUND

a lot of the time. Popo had a thing against Blue. Quit sounding like a public defender, will you? This was one of Calder's. Period."

"We pick him up now?"

"No."

"But you just said—"

"I know what I said. I know damn well what I said and I don't need a parrot to toss it back at me."

"But—"

"Shut up." I finished the coffee. "I told you Calder was a pro. You know what that means? You understand what that record says? He's a hired killer. You pay him and he shoots people. That's how he makes his living. A good living. He dresses in three hundred dollar suits. He wears gold cuff links. He lives in a penthouse overlooking Central Park. The west side of the park—he's not a millionaire. But he does well in his job."

I paused for breath. I just wanted to get home and go to bed. I was tired. "I told you about pros," I said. "They don't fool around. They don't leave loopholes. It's their business and they know it. They don't crack under pressure. If we pick up Calder he'll be out in no time at all. No witnesses. A cast-iron alibi. No holes at all."

"So what do we do?"

"We go home," I said. "We go home and take hot showers and go to bed. Tomorrow we pick him up."

I left him there to wonder what I was talking about. I went home and took a hot shower and fell asleep the minute I hit the bed.

Homicide is rugged. There are good things about it—we don't take bribes, we stay clean. There are also bad things.

Because there are only three types of murder, and of the three there is only one that we solve. There is the amateur killing with a motive, the husband who strangles his wife, the tavern brawl, the grudge murder. There you have your suspect at the start and you look around for the proof. And find it, no matter how clever a job they do of burying it. That is the kind that gets solved.

ONE NIGHT STANDS

There is also the silly killing. The bum beaten to death on the Bowery. The hustler with a knife in her belly. The fag killed in his own apartment by a casual conquest. The mugging victim with a crushed skull. These we don't solve. Not without a break.

And there is the professional murder. And those we never solve.

I met Fischer at five in the afternoon. He was carrying a folded copy of an afternoon tabloid. The headline ran GANGLAND SLAYING IN HELL'S KITCHEN. I could have guessed it word for word. I took the paper from him and gave the story a quick run-through. It was about the same as the morning papers had it.

It didn't say we had nothing to work with. It didn't say we had anything to work with. It said that Johnny Blue had been found in a parked car with holes in him, and that he was dead. Then there were a few paragraphs trying to turn the career of a fourth-rater into something notorious, and then there was some nonsense to the effect that the cops were keeping mum.

Mum?

"We're on Calder," I told him. "No other assignment until we nail him. Got that?"

"Sure."

"I wanted it that way. I want to get Calder. I want to get him good."

"I thought you said it was impossible."

"It is."

"Then—"

"You talk too much," I said. I waited for him to get mad but he didn't. He was hurt—it showed in his face, in the way he wouldn't look at me. But he wouldn't get mad. And this made me like him that much less. He never got mad at anything. He didn't know how to hate.

I don't like college cops. I don't like people who are up to their ears in understanding and sympathy and sweetness and sunshine. I don't like people who don't know how to hate.

I DON'T FOOL AROUND

Maybe it's just the way a person is. If I were Calder I would hate cops. I'm a cop. I hate Calder. I hate him because he breaks laws and shoots people. I hate him because he gets away with it. I hated Johnny Blue. He used to get away with things too. Now he was dead and Calder had killed him and I hated Calder.

I was going to get him.

"Look it over again," I said, sliding Calder's file over to Fischer again. "Skip the record. Look at the picture."

Dark black hair. A flat face, not too bad-looking. Hard eyes, a long nose, a little scar on the chin. I don't know how he got the scar. Maybe he cut himself shaving.

"You said we pick him up today. Were you kidding?"

"I don't kid. I was serious."

"They found evidence?"

"No."

He looked at me. He was afraid to open his mouth. Gutless.

"We worry him a little. Don't bother your head about it. Go get the car and meet me out front. And wear a gun."

He didn't say anything, just went off for the car. I checked my gun, then stuck it back in the holster. I picked up Calder's file, and took a good long look at it. I let the face burn into my brain. I stood there for a minute or two and hated.

Then I went out to the car where Fischer was waiting.

The building was fancy. A uniformed doorman stood at attention out in front. I had to show him my shield before he let us inside. He was there to keep out undesirables. Unless they lived in the penthouse.

The carpet was deep in the lobby. The elevator rose in silence. I stood there and hated Calder.

He had the whole top floor. I got out of the elevator and took my gun out of its holster, wondering whether or not the doorman had called Calder yet. Probably.

I rang the bell.

"Yeah?"

ONE NIGHT STANDS

A penthouse overlooking the park didn't get Hell's Kitchen out of his speech. Nothing would.

"Police."

"Whattaya want?"

"Open the door and shut up."

A few seconds later the door opened. He was short, five-six or five-seven. He was wearing a silk bathrobe and slippers that looked expensive. The apartment was well-furnished but for what he had paid he could have used an interior decorator. There was a shoddiness about the place. Maybe the shoddiness was Calder.

"Come on in," he said. "You use a drink?"

I ignored him. "You're under arrest," I told him.

"What for?"

"Murder."

"Yeah?" A wide smile. "Somebody got killed?"

"Johnny Blue."

"I'm covered," he said. No *I'm innocent* but *I'm covered*. "I was playing cards with some fellows."

"Uh-huh."

He shrugged heroically. "You want, we can go down to the station. My lawyer'll have me out right away. I'm clean."

"You're never clean," I said. "You were born filthy."

The smile widened. But there was uncertainty behind it. I was getting to him.

"You're cheap and rotten," I said. "You're a punk. You spend a fortune on cologne and it still doesn't cover the smell."

Now the smile was gone.

"Your sister sleeps with bums," I said. "Your mother was the cheapest whore on the West Side. She died of syphilis."

That did it. He was a few feet away—then he lowered his head and charged. I could have clubbed him with the gun. I didn't.

I shot him.

He gave a yell like a wounded steer and fell to his knees. The bullet had taken him in the right shoulder. I guess it hurt. I hoped so.

I DON'T FOOL AROUND

"You shot him." It was Fischer talking.

"Good thinking," I told him. "You're on the ball."

"Now what?"

I shrugged. "We can take him in," I suggested. "We can book him for resisting arrest and a few other things."

"Not murder?"

"You heard him," I said. "He's clean."

I looked at Fischer. That was the answer to my college cop, my buddy. Here was a murderer, a murderer with a shoulder wound. Now we would be nice to him. Get him to a hospital quick before he lost too much blood. Maybe drop the resisting arrest charge because, after all, he was a sick man.

I had my gun in my hand. I stepped back a few feet and aimed. I watched the play of expressions on Calder's face. He didn't know whether or not to believe it.

I shot him in the face.

I talked to Fischer while I found a gun in a drawer, picked it up in a towel and wrapped Calder's fingers around it. It made it look good—he had drawn on me, I shot him in the shoulder, he went on and held onto the gun, and I shot him dead. It would look good enough—there wasn't going to be any investigation.

"Maybe thirty killings," I said. "That's what this animal had to his credit. He made beating the law a business. He didn't fool around. And there was no way to get him."

No answer from my partner.

"So this time he lost. He doesn't fool around. Well, neither do I."

I knew Fischer wasn't satisfied. He wouldn't blab, but it would worry him. He would feel uncomfortable with me. I don't fit into his moral scheme of things. Maybe he'll put in for a transfer.

I hope so.

JUST WINDOW SHOPPING

I climbed over the back fence and hurried down the driveway. They probably hadn't seen me at the window, but I couldn't afford to take chances. The police had caught me once. I certainly did not want to be picked up again.

It was horrible when the police caught me. I admitted everything but that wasn't enough for them. They put me in a chair with the light shining in my eyes so that I could barely see. Then they started hitting me. They used rubber hoses so there wouldn't be any marks. They hit me so much I nearly fainted.

The beating wasn't the worst of it, though. They called me names. They called me a sex fiend and a pervert. That hurt me more than the beatings.

Because I'm not a pervert, you see. All I want to do is watch people. There's no harm in that, is there? I don't hurt anyone, and I never really bother anybody. Sometimes someone sees me watching them, and they get frightened or angry, but that's only once in a great while. I've been very careful lately, ever since they caught me.

And if they think I am a pervert, you should see some of the things I've seen. You wouldn't believe the things some of these normal people do. It's enough to make you sick to your stomach. Yet they are normal, and they call me a pervert, a Peeping Tom. I can't quite understand it. All I do is watch.

Ever since they caught me I have been very careful. That is why I left the window when the man looked at me. I'm almost sure he didn't see me, but he glanced toward the window and I hopped the fence and got away from there. Besides, it wasn't much fun watching at his window. The woman with him was old and fat and I was getting bored with the whole thing. There was no sense in taking chances for that.

JUST WINDOW SHOPPING

When I got out to the street I didn't know where to go. I used to have a perfect spot. A pretty young prostitute over on Tremont Avenue who saw at least ten men a night. I could spent night after night watching her. The backyard was dark and I had a perfect view. But one night she saw me watching.

She was nice about it and sensible, too. She didn't call me a pervert. But she said the men might notice me, that they wouldn't like it. She told me to stay away. It was a shame that I had to give up the spot, but at least she didn't call the police or anything.

But I couldn't watch there anymore, and I had to find a new spot. I walked down the street looking for a lighted window. I stopped at several places, but there was nothing much to see. There were just people sitting or reading or watching television.

Finally I found a house with a light on that looked promising. The back yard was dark, too, which was important. It's harder to see out from a lighted room when there is no light in the back yard.

I stood close to the window and watched. A man and woman were sitting on the bed, taking their clothes off. I watched them. The man wasn't bad looking but my attention was confined to the woman. I'm not queer, you understand.

She certainly wasn't beautiful. Better than average, though. Her face was nothing to write home about, her breasts were rather small, but she had beautiful legs and generally nice shape all in all. I watched her undress and began to get excited. This was going to be a good night after all.

They undressed quickly, which is not the way I like it. It's better when they take a good long time about it. But they just pulled off their clothes and turned down the bedcovers. I guess they had been married for some time.

I was really excited by this time, and my eyes were practically glued to the window. Then the man stood up and walked over to the wall. He touched a switch, and the room was suddenly plunged into complete darkness. I was so mad I could have killed him. Why did he have to do a thing like that.

ONE NIGHT STANDS

I stared through the window, but it was no use. The room was black as pitch. I couldn't understand it. How could he enjoy it with the lights out? He wouldn't be able to see a thing.

I was mad, and just about ready to go home and call it a night. But the little I had seen left me so excited that I could not stop there, I walked around looking for another window.

By this time it was late and I had no idea where to go. Most of the people in the neighborhood were asleep by now. But I continued walking around, hoping against hope that something would turn up.

I was just about ready to quit when I saw a lighted window on Bushnell Road. Never having been to that house before I decided to give it a try.

I approached the window and looked in. It was a bedroom window, with a woman reading there. She had her back to me, reading a magazine. She was all alone.

Ordinarily I would not have waited. Sometimes a woman will sit like that all night, just reading. But it was late and, having nowhere else to go. I waited. Besides, I had the feeling I would get a real show for my money.

As it turned out, I was right. She put down the magazine in less than five minutes, stood up, and turned toward me, I was stunned when I got a good luck at her. She was beautiful.

She was wearing a flower-print dress that made her look like a schoolgirl, but one good look at her would tell you she was nothing of the sort. Her body was far too mature for a schoolgirl's with proud, full breasts that nearly ripped the dress apart. Her face was as pretty as a model's, and her hair was that soft reddish-brown that drives me crazy. I was ready to watch her forever.

She started to undress. I stared at her greedily. There was no one else around, and my eyes studied every detail of her body. She undressed slowly, tantalizingly, slithering out of her dress and hanging it up in the closet. Finally she stood there nude, and it was worth all the waiting, worth all the walking that I had done that night. She was like a vision, the most perfect woman I had ever seen.

JUST WINDOW SHOPPING

I though I would have to go home then. I expected she would turn off the light and go to bed, and if she had I would have been satisfied. It was enough for one night. Instead she walked to her mirror and began to examine herself.

It was the perfect view for me. I could see both her back and the mirror image of her front. She looked at herself, and I watched her. Then she began to dance.

It was not exactly a dance. She moved like a burlesque dancer, but there was nothing crude about it. She knew how beautiful she was, and she moved in rhythm, making a symphony of her body and watching herself as she did. It was something to watch.

Finally she stopped dancing. She slipped on a housecoat and stepped through a door. I guessed she was going to the bathroom, which meant it was the end of the show, I could have left then, but didn't. I wanted to get another glimpse of her. She had to come back.

I stood silently at the window, waiting for her.

Suddenly a door opened. I whirled around to find her standing there, in the doorway, pointing a gun at me. "Don't move," she said. "Don't move or I'll shoot."

I froze in terror, staring down the mouth of the gun, which looked like a cannon to me. "I wasn't doing anything," I stammered. "Just watching you. I didn't hurt you."

She didn't say a word.

"Look," I pleaded, "just let me go. I won't bother you any more. I promise I'll stay away from here,"

She ignore me. "I saw you in the mirror," she said. "Saw you watching me. I danced for *you*. Did you like the way I danced?"

I nodded dumbly, unable to speak.

"It was for you," she said. "I liked your eyes on me. I liked the way you looked at me."

She smiled. "Come inside."

I hesitated, Was this a trap? Had she called the police?

"Come here," she said. "Come inside. Don't be afraid."

ONE NIGHT STANDS

I followed her into the house, into the bedroom. "I want you," she said. "I want you." She slipped out of the housecoat and tossed it over a chair.

"Come on," she aid. "I know you want me. I could tell from the way you looked at me. Come here."

She set the gun on the dresser and motioned for me to step closer. "I want you to make love to me," she said.

I walked over to her, and she threw her arms around me. "Take me," she moaned.

I pushed her away. "No," I said. "I don't want *that*. I just wanted to watch you. I wouldn't do *that*."

She pressed against me again. "I want you," she insisted. She opened her arms and I felt her hot breath on my face.

There was only one way to stop her. I picked up the gun from the dresser. "Don't come any closer," I warned. "Leave me alone."

"Don't be silly," she smiled. "You want me and I want you." She kept coming closer as I retreated.

That's when it happened—when the gun went off. The noise resounded in the small bedroom, and she crumpled and fell. "Why?" she moaned. Then she died.

The police beat me. They beat me harder than last time, and they called me a pervert. They think I tried to rape her, but that's not true. I wouldn't do a thing like that.

LIE BACK AND ENJOY IT

It was the afternoon, and the sun was beginning to dip to the level of the horizon. Frank pressed down heavily on the accelerator, gunning the car smoothly along the highway. Just a few more miles, he thought. Just a few more miles and he'd be home, if you could call an empty room in a run-down hotel home. Just a few more miles and he could take a hot bath and drink himself to sleep.

Then he saw the girl. At first glance he took her for just another hitch-hiker, and speeded up to pass her by. Then his eyes took in the long hair and the swell of the breasts, and his foot found the brake pedal and slowed the car to a stop. He reached across the front seat and opened the door.

"Hop in," he said.

She climbed into the car and sat down beside him. He took a good look then, and he liked what he saw.

She was wearing a pair of faded blue dungarees and a man's shirt, open at the throat, but even the shapeless clothing couldn't conceal the shapeliness of her figure. Her breasts were large and full, and they pressed against the flannel fabric of the shirt. Her hair was long and jetblack; her face very attractive, with high cheekbones and large brown eyes. As he looked at her, Frank felt the blood surging through his veins. He'd been a long time without a woman.

"Going to Milford?" she asked, naming a town a few miles the other side of Frank's destination.

"Sure," he said. She leaned back in the seat and closed the door, setting her small black purse on her lap.

He put the car in gear and eased back onto the highway again, watching her out of the corner of his eye. Pretty, he thought. Almost beautiful. And so very young, too—she couldn't be over 19.

"Been waiting long?" he asked.

ONE NIGHT STANDS

"Not too long. About fifteen minutes or so."

"Funny how some guys won't stop for a person, isn't it?"

"Yes," she said. "They read about people getting robbed and all, and they just drive on by."

He stole another glance at her. It took a lot for a girl to look like that in men's clothes. He pictured her in a dress, in a bathing suit, and finally in nothing at all. He turned his eyes back to the road as the perspiration began to form on his forehead.

If only he could have a girl like that! Then he wouldn't mind those damned trips all over the country, not if he had something like that back at his room, waiting for him to come home. But he couldn't have luck like that, not him. He never had.

He was 41, and his hair was starting to go. Slowly but surely, his life was slipping by, without anything real or important ever happening to him. The only love he ever had he bought for three dollars in a little room over Randy's Bar. And he knew that he would go on like that, coming home every night to an empty room and passing three dollars to a prostitute every Saturday. And someday he would die without ever doing anything.

"Mind if I smoke?" Her voice broke into his reverie and stopped his train of thought.

"Go right ahead," he said. He took a lighter from his pants pocket and turned toward her, offering her the flame.

She leaned forward to take the light. The shirt fell away from the front of her body, and Frank got a quick glimpse of smooth white skin and rounded flesh.

Again the desire surged through him. He replaced the lighter in his pocket and gripped the wheel as tight as he could in his large hands. He was breathing fast, almost panting.

"Thanks," she said, softly.

The sun dipped lower, and he passed a sign which indicated that his town was only two miles further on down the road. Just two more miles, then three or four to Milford, and she would be gone from his

LIE BACK AND ENJOY IT

life. She would leave, and he would be left with her memory and nothing more.

He looked at her again. She seemed so soft, so warm and peaceful. She yawned and stretched her lush body before him. And then he decided that he was going to have her.

The decision came in a flash. He couldn't let his whole life disappear without doing something about it. He would take her, swiftly and violently; and the freshness of her would let him live again like a full man.

The realization of what he was going to do calmed him. At the same time, he was tense with anticipation. He could practically feel the soft pressure of her body against his, could picture her nude in his arms.

"Just a few more miles," she said.

"Won't be long now." He turned and smiled at her.

"I really appreciate this. It'd be terrible out on the road at night."

I'm glad you appreciate it, he thought. You'll get a chance to show just how grateful you are. A good chance.

He didn't really want to hurt her. He glanced over at her again. Hell, he thought, she was no virgin. It wasn't as though he were taking something away from her. She might even like it. He chuckled inwardly, remembering the old saying, "If rape is inevitable, lie back and enjoy it."

Well, it was inevitable. He was going to take her, and nothing was going to stop him. He wouldn't hurt her anymore than he had to, of course. Maybe she would tell the police, but he was willing to take the chance. He couldn't stop himself now, even if he wanted to.

Besides, there was little chance that she would tell. He had read somewhere that 90 % of the rape cases were never reported, because the girls involved were ashamed of it. And he could always say that she let him—no one could prove otherwise.

"It's a nice day," he said.

"Very nice."

ONE NIGHT STANDS

He spotted a turn-off, a rutted, two-lane road that went nowhere and was rarely used by anyone. He slowed down the car and cut over onto it.

"Where are we going?" she asked. There was a touch of alarm in her voice.

"A short cut," he replied.

"I never went this way before."

"It cuts out Herkinsburg. Not many people know about it."

He was amazed to hear himself lie so easily. He had always had difficulty in lying, but now he was so set on his goal that the words came from his lips with no trouble at all. Evidently she believed him, for she relaxed in the seat.

After a few hundred yards on the turn-off, he cut the motor and pulled the car over to the shoulder of the road. It was time, now. No one would disturb them.

"Why are we stopping?" There was panic in her voice now, as she sat up rigidly and gripped the black purse tight in both hands.

He didn't answer. His right hand encircled both her wrists in a tight grip; his left shoved the car door open. Then he forced her out of the car. The purse flew from her hands as he sent her sprawling to the ground and flung himself upon her.

"No!" she pleaded. "Don't!" His face was so close to hers that he could feel her breath against his cheek, just as he could feel the warmth of her body through the thin shirt.

"You can't stop me," he said. "No one'll hear you if you scream." He smiled. "You might as well lie back and enjoy it."

At last it was over. The girl remained motionless.

"There," he said. "That wasn't so bad, was it?"

She didn't answer. He walked slowly back to the car, taking deep breaths of air and savoring the taste of it in his lungs.

He had one hand on the door-handle when he heard her say, "Stop!" There was something in her voice that compelled him to release the door-handle and turn around.

LIE BACK AND ENJOY IT

She was holding the small black purse in one hand and a small black automatic in the other. The gun was trained on him.

"You bastard," she said. "I was just going to take your car, I would even have left you a little money to get home on, but not now."

His mouth dropped open in shock. "Wait," he stammered. "Wait a minute."

"You can't stop me," she said, levelly. "I'm going to kill you. You might as well lie back and enjoy it."

The bullet made a small, round hole in his stomach. He fell on the ground and lay there moaning while she straightened her clothes and took the wallet and keys from his pockets. He watched her get into the car, blow him a kiss, and drive away down the road.

It took him twenty minutes to die.

LOOK DEATH IN THE EYE

She was beautiful.

She was, and she knew that she was—not only by the image in her mirror, the full and petulant mouth and the high cheekbones, the silkiness of the long blond hair and the deep blue colour of her eyes. The image in her mirror at home told her she was beautiful, and so did the image she saw now, the image in the mirror in the tavern.

But she didn't need the mirrors. She was made aware of her beauty by the eyes, the eyes of the hungry men, the eyes that she felt rather than saw upon her everywhere she went. She could feel those eyes caressing her body, lingering too long upon her firm ripe breasts and sensuous hips, touching her body with a touch firmer than hands and making her grow warm where they rested. Wherever she went men stared at her, and the intensity of their stares undressed their passions and hungers just as thoroughly as the stares attempted to strip her body.

She sipped at her drink, hardly tasting it but knowing that she had to drink it. It was all part of the game. She was in a bar, and the hungry men were also in the bar, and now their eyes were wondering over her. But for the moment there was nothing for her to do. She had to drink her drink and bide her time, waiting for the men—or one of them, at least—to get up the courage to do more than stare.

Idly, she turned a few inches on the bar stool and glanced at the other customers. Several men were too busy drinking to pay any attention to her; another was busy in a corner booth running his hand up and down the leg of a slightly-plump redhead, and it was easy to see that he wouldn't be interested in her, not that night.

But the other three customers were fair game.

She regarded them thoughtfully, one at a time. Closest to her was a young one—no more than 21 or 22, she guessed, and hungry the

LOOK DEATH IN THE EYE

way they are when they're that age. He was short and slim, dressed in a dark suit and wearing a conservative bow-tie. She noticed with a little amusement the way he was embarrassed to stare at her but at the same time was unable to keep his eyes off her lush body. Twice his eyes met hers and he flushed guiltily, turning away and nervously flicking the ashes off his cigarette.

And each time the eyes returned to her, hungry and desperate in their hunger. Mr. Dark Suit couldn't keep away from her, she thought, and she wondered if he would be the one for the evening. It was always difficult to predict, always tough to calculate which pair of eyes would get up enough courage to make the pass. It might be Mr. Dark Suit, but she doubted it. He had the hunger, all right, but he probably lacked the experience he'd need for hero.

Mr. Baldy was two stools further from her. She named him easily since his baldness was his outstanding feature in a face that had no other memorable features. His head was bare except for a very thin fringe around the edges and the light from the ceiling shined on it.

Next, of course, she noticed his eyes. They were hungry eyes, too —but hungry in a way that was different from Mr. Dark Suit. Mr. Baldy was a good 25 years older, and he was probably used to getting his passes tossed back into his lap. He wanted her, all right; there was no mistaking the intensity of his gaze. But the possibility of a refusal might scare him away.

For a half-second she considered flashing him a smile. No, she decided, that wouldn't be fair. Let them work it out themselves. Let the hungriest assert himself and the others forever hold their peace.

And there was no hurry. It was rather a pleasant feeling to be caressed simultaneously by three pairs of eyes, and though the sensation was hardly a new one, it was one she never tired of.

And the third man. He was seated at the far end of the bar, seated so that he could study her without turning at all. But, strangely, his eyes were not glued to her body the way Mr. Dark Suit's and Mr. Baldy's were. Instead he was relaxing, biding his time, and

ONE NIGHT STANDS

occasionally letting his eyes wander from his beer-glass to her and back to his beer.

He was somewhere in his thirties, with a strong and vaguely handsome face and jet-black hair. Mr. Bright-Eyes, she named him, laughing inwardly at the glow of assurance and confidence in his eyes.

Mr. Bright-Eyes wouldn't be afraid or stumbling about it. At the same time, she wondered whether or not he would care enough to make an approach. He wanted her; that much she knew. But he might need a little shove in the right direction.

A rock-and-roll tune was playing noisily on the juke box. *Not yet*, she thought. *Wait until everything is just right, with soft music and all the trimmings. Let the eyes stay hungry for a few minutes.*

She studied them again, the three of them. Mr. Dark Suit's eyes, she noticed, were brown. Mr. Baldy's eyes were a watery blue, a bit bloodshot and sick-looking. But Mr. Bright-Eyes had, happily, bright blue eyes. They seemed to gleam in his powerful face.

She wondered who it would be. Another night, another pair of eyes—but who would it be tonight? Which eyes were the hungriest? Which eyes wanted her, wanted her enough to hurry up and make a pass?

Mr. Dark-Suit finished his drink and signaled the bar tender for another. He sipped at it nervously when it arrived, then set it down on the bar and stole another glance at her, drumming his fingers on the bar all the while.

He's so nervous, she thought. *If I made the first move he'd come running. But he's scared silly.*

Mr. Baldy, his drink forgotten, stared at her quite openly. He didn't seem shy at all, and the watery blue eyes moved up and down her body without the slightest embarrassment.

He can watch, she thought. *A looker, but not much for action. What's the matter, Mr. Baldy?*

LOOK DEATH IN THE EYE

Mr. Bright-Eyes looked up from his beer and saw her studying him. For a moment a shadow of a smile passed over his face; then it was gone, and he was gazing once again into the glass of beer.

Although she wanted to be perfectly fair, she felt herself hoping that it would be Mr. Bright-Eyes. She always played perfectly fair, always went with the first one, but this time she felt a decided preference. There was something about those eyes, something about the way they looked at her so openly . . .

The rock-and-roll tune came to a noisy finish. She waited on her stool, fluffing her hair into place and taking another short sip of her drink.

The next record was a slow one.

Now, she thought. First she stretched a little, throwing her shoulders back so that her two perfect breasts stood out in bold relief as they pressed against the thin fabric of her blouse. Then she crossed one leg over the other, letting her skirt fall away as she did so and giving Mr. Dark Suit and Mr. Baldy a quick glimpse of milk-white skin.

Unfortunately, Mr. Bright-Eyes couldn't see her legs from where he sat. It was a pity.

Then, with her breasts jutting and her legs crossed, she tossed off the rest of her drink and leaned forward on her stool, hesitating a moment before ordering a refill. This was the crucial moment, the time when one of the three had to be ready for a game of drop-the-handkerchief. Somebody had to pick up the cue.

"Another beer for me, and one more for the lady."

She started, turned her head, and discovered happily that it was Mr. Bright-Eyes. He certainly was smooth, she marveled, the way he was right at her side the minute she was ready for another drink.

A moment later the beer was poured, the drink made, and Mr. Bight-Eyes seated on the stool beside her. She noticed the sad looks in the eyes of Mr. Baldy and Mr. Dark Suit, sad because they realized the chance they had missed.

ONE NIGHT STANDS

Too bad, she thought. *You had your chances. Why, you had a better chance than Mr. Bright-Eyes, what with looking at my legs and all.*

"You're a lovely woman," Mr. Bright-Eyes was saying, and she was pleased to note that he had a fine manner of speaking, spacing his words nicely and pronouncing all the consonants the way they belonged. Why, that man a few nights ago didn't talk very well at all, mumbling the way he did. Of course it was partly the drinking, but she was glad Mr. Bright-Eyes could speak so clearly and nicely.

But she didn't pay much attention to what he was saying. It wasn't too important, and besides she was far too busy looking into his blue eyes and enjoying the way they traveled so gently over her body. She could feel them on her, and when his gaze traveled down her body and caressed her hips she almost shivered.

He continued to talk to her and she continued to answer him and the juke box continued to play, but she spent most of her time looking into his eyes and loving the feeling they gave her. He told her his name, which she promptly forgot because Mr. Bright-Eyes suited him so much better, and she told him that her name wasn't especially important, since it really wasn't.

Mr. Bright-Eyes said something about a rose by another name and she laughed politely, but it was his eyes that really held her interest. Even when his hand moved down to rest gently on her thigh, she was more aware of the hunger in his eyes than the gradually more insistent pressure of his hand.

Slowly his hand moved up and down her thigh, gently caressing her flesh, and all the while Mr. Bright-Eyes was talking earnestly, his voice just a little louder than a whisper and his eyes deliciously lustful and hungry.

But it wouldn't do to ignore the hand. Keeping her gaze rooted to Mr. Bright-Eye's face, she gently placed her own hand on top of his. At first he seemed taken aback, thinking that she wished him to remove his hand from her thigh. That, of course, was not what she intended at all.

LOOK DEATH IN THE EYE

Reassuringly, she moved his hand over her thigh, pressing it gently and tenderly. She was pleased to notice Mr. Bright-Eyes get an even hungrier gleam in his eyes and begin to breathe a slight bit heavier than before. It was all part of the game, but the game could be very pleasant for her.

". . . one of the most exciting women I've ever met," he was saying, and as he spoke the words his hand closed possessively around her knee. His eyes were glued to her breasts. She knew that they would leave any moment now, that he was almost ready and almost convinced that she would now follow him to the ends of the earth if he were only to ask.

And indeed she would.

"Honey?"

She smiled expectantly.

"Would you like to have the next one up at my place?"

"Of course," she said.

His bright blue eyes gleamed more than ever. How bright they were! She was actually in love with him now, in love with his eyes and the hunger and beauty in them.

As they stood up, she saw Mr. Baldy shake his head sadly. Mr. Dark Suit's jaw fell slightly and he looked quite awkward, sitting precariously on his stool with his mouth half-open. Then Mr. Bright-Eyes slipped his arm easily around her waist and walked her to the door. She could feel their eyes watching her every step of the way, and it wasn't hard at all to imagine the regret in their eyes—regret mixed with admiration for Mr. Bright-Eye's technique.

He was smooth, all right. So very smooth, and while it was a shame that Mr. Dark Suit and Mr. Baldy were doomed to sadness for the evening, it simply couldn't be helped.

And besides, wasn't there a book about survival of the fittest or something? If they had Mr. Bright-Eyes' finish they wouldn't be sitting by themselves, with their eyes all afraid and beaten.

It was dark out, and Mr. Bright-Eyes seemed to be in a hurry, and as a consequence they were walking very swiftly toward his

ONE NIGHT STANDS

apartment. He said something about wasn't it dark out, and she agreed that it was, and his arm tightened around her waist.

She leaned a little against him and rubbed her body against his. Walking as they were and with the night as dark as it was, it was hard for her to see his eyes. Each time when they passed a streetlamp she leaned forward a bit and glanced into his face, as if to reassure herself that his eyes still wanted her as much as they had.

In his apartment everything went very well. He told her how beautiful she was and she thanked him quite modestly, and they went to the bedroom and he took her in his arms and kissed her very expertly.

Then, after she had been expertly kissed, he bent over to remove the spread from the bed. It was at just that moment that she took the knife from her purse and plunged it into his back, right between the shoulder blades. One jab was enough; he crumpled up on the bed and lay very still, without a scream or a moan or any sound at all.

Afterwards, back in her own apartment, she put his eyes in the box with the others.

MAN WITH A PASSION

He set his suitcase down on the floor in front of the desk, then unslung the leather bag from his shoulder and placed it beside the suitcase. He smiled across the desk at the clerk, an easy, automatic smile. "I'd like a room," he said. "With bath."

The clerk nodded wordlessly and passed the hotel register to the man. He uncapped a pen and began filling in the blanks. *Jacob Falch,* he wrote. *Free-lance photographer.* He hesitated a moment before the last blank, then quickly scrawled *No permanent address.* He paid in advance, took a key from the clerk, and carried his luggage up the steep staircase to his room.

He was a short man, with broad shoulders and a rough, craggy face. He walked swiftly and purposefully, carrying the bag with ease despite its weight. He reached his room, turned the key in the lock, and seated himself heavily on the bed.

The room was drab and colorless. There was the bed, a straight-backed chair that looked as though it would buckle if he sat on it, and a dull-brown dresser studded with cigarette burns. In short, Falch reflected, it was a crummy room in a cheap hotel. But it would do for the time being.

He started to lie down for a nap, then changed his mind and began to unpack the suitcase. His camera supplies—flash-bulbs, filters, chemicals, and film—he placed in the bottom drawer of the dresser. He hung his suit in the small closet, noting with satisfaction that the pants still held a crease. His shirts and other clothing went into the middle bureau drawer. Only one small package remained in the suitcase, and he took it out and held it lovingly in his large hands. It was a very important package. It contained ten thousand dollars.

Ten thousand dollars, he thought, and he chuckled softly. He'd had to work hard for the money. Any hack photographer could

ONE NIGHT STANDS

plaster a composite picture together, but it took skill to make one that would stick. It took plenty of skill to come up with a batch of shots that put the mayor's wife in a compromising position. A very compromising position, he reflected, and chuckled once again.

The mayor had paid through the nose, but the mayor could afford it. And the mayor could definitely not afford to have his opponents get hold of those pictures. His wife seemed to be doing things that a mayor's wife shouldn't do. Very interesting things.

Falch chuckled again, and patted the packet of money tenderly. Of course he'd had to leave town, but Tarleton was a dull town anyway. And with ten thousand in his suitcase he could go far.

No more portraits, he thought. No more squirming brats in family groups, no more dirty pictures for backroom boys, no more publicity shots of fertilizer plants. For once in his life Jake Falch could do what he damn well wanted.

And Jake Falch knew what he wanted. Plenty of relaxation, for one thing. Decent food, and a woman now and then. His tastes were inexpensive enough, and he could be very happy in the dumpy hotel, with his battered coupe parked outside.

Oh, he'd take pictures now and then. A little cheesecake, if there was a decent-looking broad in the town. And, when the money ran out . . . well, every town had a mayor, and every mayor had a wife. Or a daughter. Or a sister.

He looked around the room for a hiding place for the money. No, he realized, that was senseless. It would be hard hiding a toothpick in that place, let alone a nice thick wad of bills. And, since he was staying in town, he might as well bank his dough, like a respectable businessman. He chuckled again, and left the room.

The desk clerk stopped him on the way out. "You a photographer, Mr. Falch?"

Falch nodded.

"Figure on staying in town?"

Falch nodded again, impatiently.

"You'll need a studio, a darkroom. Brother of mine has a place. . ."

MAN WITH A PASSION

"No," said Falch, cutting him short. "I won't be working for awhile. Came into some money and I feel like taking it easy." He smiled again, the same easy smile he had flashed to the Mayor, and walked out the door. The bank was across the street, on the corner.

Five minutes later he strode out of the bank, with $9500 in a checking account. He breathed deeply and headed across the street again to a restaurant. He felt good.

I t was then that be saw the girl. She was walking toward him on the other side of the street, and even a half-block away he could see that she was beautiful. She was young—18 or 19, he guessed—and she had soft, shining blond hair that fell to her shoulders and framed her face perfectly. Automatically, Falch placed her face inside a mental picture frame.

By the time he reached the restaurant, the girl was within twenty yards of him. He saw that her body was a perfect match for her face. It was the kind of body he liked, with full, round curves. It was a lush body, a young body.

Just as he had placed her face inside a frame, he mentally undressed her. He let his eyes run over her body, lingering on the firm, jutting breasts and the rounded hips. Guiltily, he tried to turn away and enter the restaurant, but before he could move she had walked right up to him.

"Hi," she said. "You're new in town, aren't you?" Her voice was as soft and as fresh as the rest of her. She'd make a good model, he thought. She had a face and a figure, and that was a rare combination.

He smiled then, the wide, friendly smile that came so easily to him. "That's right. My name's Jake Falch."

"Mine's Saralee Marshall. Are you the photographer?"

He blinked. "How did you know?"

"Jimmy at the hotel told my Ma, and Ma told me. I figured you must be the photographer, because not many strangers ever come to Hammondsport." She made the name of the town sound like a dirty word.

ONE NIGHT STANDS

He smiled again. "You don't like this town?"

"Oh," she said, "I guess it's okay. But it's so awful dull. Nothing ever happens, hardly."

"Where would you like to live?"

She shrugged her shoulders, and her breasts rose and fell with the motion. "New York, maybe. Or Hollywood."

"You want to be an actress, huh?"

"No," she said. "I want to be a model."

He had to catch his breath, and before he could get a word out she was off a mile a minute. "I wonder if you need a model? I'd work hard, Mr. Falch. Honest I would. There's no school all summer and I could work whenever you wanted me to and I know I don't have any experience but I can learn real well and. . ."

"Hold on a minute!" He laughed and held up his hand up. "I don't know how much I could pay you. . ."

"You don't have to pay me. Just for the experience, it would be worth it." Her eyes pleaded with him, and it was all he could do to keep from laughing out loud. He'd pay ten bucks an hour for a gal like her, any day of the week.

"Well," he said, forcing himself to hesitate, "I guess we could give it a try. But you might not like modeling; I mean, you might not like to pose for, well. . ."

She smiled. "You mean cheesecake? I don't mind. Whatever you want."

Whatever he wanted! If only she knew what he wanted, what plans he had for her. He looked over her body again, drinking in the vibrance of it. Paula must have been like that, once. It had been good with Paula, and he could almost feel the way it would be with Saralee.

"Saralee," he said, aloud, "where would you like to work? I don't have a studio yet."

"How about outside? There is a little stream down the road, no good for swimming or fishing. Nobody goes there, so it's a perfect spot. Nice scenery too. Kind of wild, like."

MAN WITH A PASSION

"Fine," said Falch. "I'll pick you up tomorrow morning, in front of the hotel. 11:30 okay?"

"Wonderful. Oh, I can hardly wait!" She turned, then, and half-ran, half-walked down the street. Falch stood rooted to the spot watching her.

When he left the hotel the next morning his camera bag over his shoulder, she was waiting for him. She wore a gray skirt that hugged her hips and a tight yellow sweater that threatened to burst any minute. He led her to the car, and they drove off down the road to the spot she had picked out.

It was, as she had said, a perfect spot. The tough wooden bridge and thick-trunked oak provided a rustic touch, which contrasted sharply with the green of the grass and the blue water. Falch wished fleetingly that he had brought color film.

He was a good photographer, and he worked swiftly. He posed her in a variety of spots—leaning lazily against the bridge, sitting at the base of the tree, staring moodily into the water. He taught her how to pose, how to smile, and she was a good pupil. Falch was surprised to discover that his interest in the pictures was almost as great as his desire for Saralee.

He was careful not to try any real cheesecake that first day. He did take a few leg shots, but he kept her fully clothed and avoided the more provocative poses. Saralee attracted him more than any girl he could remember, and he didn't want to spoil things at the start. She was so young and inexperienced, he'd have to play things very slowly. And he had all the time in the world.

Getting into the car for the ride back, she brushed against him accidentally, and the softness of her skin startled him and sent his pulse up. He wanted to reach for her, then and there, but he forced himself to bide his time.

At night, he covered the cracks and light openings in his room with masking tape and developed the pictures. They were better than he had expected. The girl could project herself, could endow the

ONE NIGHT STANDS

pictures with real vitality. He thought how she would be in his arms, with her blonde hair spread over a pillow.

Gradually, day by day, he took increasingly sexier pictures of her. He taught her to bring her body into harmony with the camera. He photographed her in a skimpy bathing suit, with the sun glistening on her flawless skin. He posed her in a low-cut gown that he bought just for that purpose, and with her blouse open part way down the front, so that it barely hid her breasts. That time he could barely stand it, and beads of sweat dotted his forehead.

Saralee took it all in stride. She never faltered, accepting it all as part of the job of becoming a model. She showed more and more of her legs and breasts, and never so much as blushed.

"Don't you have a boyfriend?" he'd asked one day.

"I used to go with Tom Larson, but not anymore. He's too young for me. Maybe you met him," she'd added. "He works at the drug store."

Falch remembered the boy—thin, with pimples on his face. He would be no problem at all.

And then one day, when the curves of her breasts and belly and thighs filled him with a desire he couldn't suppress, he knew that the time had come. "Saralee," he said, "I think we ought to try something a little bit different. Unless you'd rather not."

She looked at him. "Nudes? Is that what you mean, Jake?"

"Well..."

"I think that would be nice," she said, smiling sweetly. "I mean, all the top models did nude shots first, didn't they?"

He nodded, breathing heavily. "I'd love to," she said. "But we can't do that *here,* Jake. Somebody might see, and besides, there's a law against it."

"Maybe at my room, in the hotel."

"Wait," she said. "I have a better idea. How about my house?"

He stared at her incredulously. "Your house? But your folks..."

"They're out of town for the weekend. Could you come up about nine?"

118

MAN WITH A PASSION

It was better than he'd dared to hope for. The clerk might be nosey at the hotel, and if she got rough it might be noisy. But at her house there'd be no worries. "Nine," he said. "I'll be there."

He was there early, and when she stood nude before him he felt that he had never seen anything so beautiful in his life. There was not a hint of shyness about her, just pride and pleasure in her own loveliness. He began taking pictures.

After he'd shot a roll of film, he took a pint of whiskey from his camera-bag. "This calls for a celebration," he explained. "Your first nude shots. We have to have a few drinks."

She protested weakly that she had never had whiskey before, but gave in without much argument. They had a drink each, then shot another roll, and then had another round of drinks.

It was easy to see that she was unaccustomed to alcohol. A glow came into her cheeks and her eyes became even brighter than usual. They went on drinking and taking pictures, and he knew that he was almost ready to take her.

When he posed her, he let his hands linger longer than necessary upon her smooth skin, and he felt the heat building up within her. She breathed faster, deeper. It was time.

He said nothing; he didn't have to. He set down the camera, switched off the lights, and took her by the hand. His right arm encircled her waist, his hand stroking the soft flesh of her belly. He led her down the hall, to the darkened bedroom, and disrobed swiftly. His hands raced over her body, he pressed a long hard kiss upon her lips, and then he took her.

When the morning sunlight filtered through the venetian blinds, Falch rolled over and swore softly. His mind filled with memories of the night and he chuckled to himself. God, she bad been good! Fresh and new and hot as a stove. And she had enjoyed it as much as he had.

He turned over to look at her, but the bed was empty. Must be cooking up some breakfast, he thought, chuckling. Breakfast in bed.

ONE NIGHT STANDS

It had taken a lot of hard work, but you didn't get things like that easily. And she had been worth it. He had a good life to look forward to now, with no more fooling around. He'd have her whenever he wanted.

"Saralee!" he called. "Saralee!"

Seconds later the door opened. But it was not Saralee. It was a boy.

"Who the hell are you?" Falch demanded. Then he took a closer look, and he recognized him. It was Tom Larson, the boy from the drugstore.

The boy smiled, and it was a smile very much like Falch's. "Shut up," he said. "You just keep quiet there, Mr. Falch."

Falch gaped at him, unable to utter a sound.

"Got a surprise for you," said Tom. He reached into a pocket of his jeans and pulled out a picture, passing it to Falch.

Falch stared at the picture and his mouth fell open. "Got lots more like that," the boy said. "Took 'em last night, a whole mess of pictures. They're going to cost you, Mr. Falch."

The boy tapped the picture significantly. "Nice and clear, huh? Saralee's a good little model, Mr. Falch. And only 17, too. A nice respectable girl like that, it's going to cost you plenty. They're rough on guys like you in this state."

He pulled the picture from Falch's hand and studied it, grinning with satisfaction.

"Came out perfect, the whole batch of 'em. Used infra-red film and a fast shutter. Just stood in the closet and snapped 'em off. Didn't need a drop of light."

The boy laughed. "But I don't need to explain all that to you, Mr. Falch. Hell, I bet you're an old hand at this sort of thing!"

MURDER IS MY BUSINESS

I live in a poorly furnished room a block off the Bowery. I used to live there because I couldn't afford anything better. But times have changed. I live there now because I like it. It's almost cozy, once you get used to it. The smells stop bothering you after the first week or so, and the people down there never bother anybody. The other tenants are upper-caste prostitutes. The winos are always drunk and the prostitutes are always available. I like the set-up.

It's also a good business location. I live in my room, and I run my business from the bar a few doors down the street. Some of my clients don't like the neighborhood, but they manage to come here anyhow. They need me more than I need them. Business has been good this year.

I was sitting in the bar at my usual table in the back looking at a beer and watching it get warm. It was the middle of the afternoon, and I never drink before dinner. Eddie doesn't like me to sit without drinking, so I usually buy a beer or two during the afternoon and watch it go flat. I was reading a book of Spanish poetry when she came in.

I knew right off she was a prospective client. Women like her don't hang out in Skid Row bars. They were either kept in penthouses or married to Scarsdale millionaires. You could tell from one look at her.

It wasn't just that she was beautiful, but that was a part of it. The women who live here have used up their best years on Eighth Avenue, and all the flavor has gone out of them. They all drank too much, and most of them have scars on their faces from men who drank too much. And they walk with a what-the-Hell shuffle. The women on the Bowery aren't beautiful, and this one was.

ONE NIGHT STANDS

She had blonde hair, and not the kind that comes out of a bottle. It was cut short, and curled around a very passable face. She was wearing a suit, but it couldn't hide her body. It was a more than passable body.

But as I said, it was more than her beauty. She had class, and that is something which never winds its way to the Bowery. It's something you can't pin down, but it's the visible difference between Nashua and the horse that pulls Benny's peanut wagon. This babe had class.

She walked in as though she had every right to be there, and every eye in the place turned to her. They didn't watch her for long, though. The people who hang out in Eddie's Bar are only interested in wine, and a woman is something which just stirs up memories.

She looked around for a minute, and finally met my stare. She came over and I pointed to a chair. She sat down, and we stared at each other for awhile.

"Are you the man?"

It was a hell of an opener, so I played it cool and asked her just what man she was talking about.

"The man who . . . does jobs for people."

"That depends," I said. "What kind of job?" I was enjoying this.

"Couldn't we go someplace more private?"

I shook my head. "Nobody listens here," I said. "And if they do, they won't remember. And if they remember, they won't care. So speak up."

"A man told me you . . . killed people." It was an effort for her to get the words out.

I asked her what man, and she described Al. That meant a quick ten percent for Al, and it also meant that the chick was an honest customer.

"Did he tell you my fee?"

"He said five hundred dollars."

I nodded. "Do you have it?" This time she nodded. "Well," I said, "Whom do you want taken care of?"

MURDER IS MY BUSINESS

"My husband," she said. "He found out I was playing around and he's cutting me out of his will."

That was standard enough. "Okay," I said. "When do you want the job done?"

"Is tonight too soon?"

"Tonight is fine," I said. "Give me the address." She did and it wasn't Scarsdale, but Riverside Drive came to about the same thing. I memorized it quickly.

"Okay," I said. "I'll be up about 9:30."

"Fine," she said. "I'll go out."

I shook my head. "Stay home. What do you usually do nights?"

She nearly blushed. "Watch television," she said. "My husband is old."

I could see why she wanted to kill him. A woman like her needed to be loved plenty. She was wasted on an old guy.

I got back to business. "Stay home tonight," I said. "Watch television. I'll make like a burglar and take care of him, then you give me time to get away and call the cops. That way if I should get picked up, you can say I wasn't the murderer. Get it?"

She nodded. I asked for the cash, and she passed it to me under the table. I gave it a quick count and pocketed it.

"Fine," I said. "I'll see you tonight." I waited for her to get up and leave, but she didn't move.

"You're young for this business aren't you?" I almost broke out laughing.

"Not that young," I said. "It beats petty larceny."

She kept looking at me. "What's your name?" she asked.

"I haven't got one," I said. It was the truth. I had had ten names in the past year-and-a-half, and I was between aliases at the moment.

She was still staring at me. "Do you live around here?"

"Yes."

"Take me to your room."

ONE NIGHT STANDS

I hadn't expected it, but it wasn't a shock. I stood up, threw a dime on the table for the beer, and led the way. She didn't say a word.

When we reached my room I discovered I had been right—the suit couldn't hide her perfection.

When she left, still without a word, I lay on my back staring at the cracks in the ceiling. Tonight would be a pleasure. Bodies like that should not be wasted on rich old men. I felt like a public servant.

I dressed again and went back to the bar, reclaiming my table and watching another beer get flat. I read some more of the Spanish poetry, but it was anti-climatic. I had made love to a poem, and the printed page cannot compete with that.

Then he came in, and I saw he was another client. He looked no more at home in Eddie's Bar than she had. He looked a little like my Uncle Charlie, and I liked him right off. He didn't hesitate, but came right over and sat down.

"I have a job for you," he said. "Al sent me. Here's your fee and the address of the party in question." He slipped an envelope under the table, and I pocketed it.

"I'll be home," he said. "In case they ever pick you up, I'll refuse to identify you. Force an entrance, do your job, and leave."

He was one hell of a guy, businessman right down the line. I don't normally enjoy people telling me the way to operate, but I didn't mind it coming from him. He was sharp.

I nodded, and asked him when he wanted the job done.

"Tonight," he said.

I shook my head. "I can't make it," I said. "How's tomorrow?"

"Tonight," he said. "It has to be tonight."

I thought for a minute. I didn't relish the idea of two jobs in one night. It just doubled the chances of getting caught. But I could use the money, and I knew I couldn't stall him. "All right," I said. "I'm not sure on the time, but I'll make it tonight."

MURDER IS MY BUSINESS

He didn't waste any time. He stood up and left. The heads in the bar followed him until he reached the door, then returned to their glasses of port. I returned to the Spanish poetry.

I read for about an hour, threw another dime on the table, and left. I walked up to my room, placed the money in a strongbox, and put two hundred dollars into my wallet. I'd need two guns tonight, one for each job. I hoped that Sam had them on hand.

Then I glanced at the address and flushed the slip of paper and the envelope down the hall toilet. I walked downstairs, and I got all the way to Sam's hockshop before it hit me.

I bought one gun. I bought a Luger with a silencer, and loaded it. It cost one hundred dollars across the counter, with no record of sale.

Sam was a good businessman himself. I could be sure that the gun would never be traced to me, and that was important. I made it back to my room and ate dinner.

Dinner was the usual—three fried eggs and two cups of black coffee. I live on eggs and coffee. It's cheap and nourishing, and I like it. I suppose I could afford caviar if I wanted it, but I'd rather let the money accumulate in the strongbox.

You see, a real businessman never worries about the money. He doesn't care about spending it, and he doesn't count up the pennies. The money's just the chips in the pokerpot, just something to keep score with. A real businessman is interested in running a straight business, and he gets his kicks out of the business itself. A real businessman is along the lines of an artist. And I am a business man. I do a clean job. It's the way I like to live.

I finished the meal and washed up the dishes. I didn't feel much like reading, so I sat around thinking. I had come a long way from the days when I used to steal food and swindle hockshops for a couple of bucks at a time. I was established in business, and the competition was nothing to speak of. I could raise my prices sky-high, and I'd still have more work than I could handle. There's a remarkable shortage of free-lance gunmen in town.

ONE NIGHT STANDS

I sat around till 8:30 and then caught the subway to Times Square. I transferred to the Broadway IRT train there, and got off at 96th Street. It was a short walk to Riverside Drive.

The elevator was a self-service one, which cut down the chances of an identification. I rode to the top floor and rang the bell.

He answered it with a smile on his face. I walked in, and noticed that the television was on good and loud. He hadn't realized that I used a silencer.

I closed the door, took the gun from my pocket, and shot him. The bullet caught him in the side of the head and he didn't have time to be surprised. He fell like an ox.

She jumped up and came to me. She was wearing a skirt and sweater this time, and I could see every bit of that body. She was the kind of woman I could fall in love with, if I believed in love. But in my business I can't afford to.

I leveled the gun again and squeezed the trigger. Her eyes opened in horror before the bullet hit her, but she didn't have time to scream. I shot her in the head, and she died immediately.

It was a shame I had to kill her. But I had made an agreement, and I stick to my word even if my client is a corpse. Business is business.

ONE NIGHT OF DEATH

It was just seven o'clock. I heard the bells ring at the little church two blocks down Mercer Street, and the bells set me on edge.

Seven o'clock.

In five hours they would kill my father.

They would take him from his cell and walk slowly to a little room at the end of the corridor. It would be a long walk, but it would end with him inside the little room, alone, with the door closed after him. Then he would sit or stand or wait.

At precisely twelve o'clock, they'd open the gas vents. The cyanide gas would rush into the chamber. Maybe he'd cough; I didn't know. But whether he did or not, the gas would enter his lungs when he breathed. Oh, he'd try to hold his breath as long as he could. My dad's a fighter, you see, but there are some things you can't fight.

The gas would kill him. Then they would draw the gas back into the tanks to save it for the next one, and they'd take my father's body out of the room. It would be buried somewhere.

I couldn't stay in the house another minute. I couldn't sit watching my mother try to dull the pain with glass after glass of cheap muscatel, couldn't listen to her crying softly. I wanted to cry, too—but I didn't know how any more.

I slipped on my jacket and left the house, closing the door softly. It was cool outside. The air was crisp and fresh, with a breeze blowing and the fallen leaves skittering along the pavement.

It could have been a beautiful night, but it wasn't.

My father was a murderer, and tonight they were going to kill him.

Murderer. The picture that word makes isn't right at all. Because my dad's not a cruel or a vicious man or a money-hungry man. He was a cutter in a dress-shop, not too long ago, and he saved his

ONE NIGHT STANDS

money so that he could go into business for himself in the Seventh Avenue rat-race.

It was no place for him, a mild, easy-going guy. The law of the Avenue is kill or be killed, screw the competition before they screw you. But dad didn't want to hand anyone a raw deal. He just wanted to make pretty dresses and sell them. And Seventh Avenue isn't like that, not at all.

He managed to stomach it. It kept us eating good and he managed to make the kind of dresses he wanted. A man can learn to adjust to almost anything, he told me once. A man does what he has to do.

Dad's partner was a man named Bookspan, and he handled the business end while dad took care of production. Bookspan was a crook, and the one thing dad couldn't adjust to was a crooked partner, a partner who was cheating him.

When dad found out, he killed him.

Not impulsively, with the anger hot and fresh in him, because he's not an impulsive sort of man. He bided his time and waited, until he and Bookspan took a business trip to Los Angeles. He picked up a pistol in a hockshop in L.A. and blew out Bookspan's brains.

And they caught him, of course. The poor guy, he didn't even try to get away. It was an open-and-shut case, premeditated and all. He was tried in L. A. where the murder took place, and he was sentenced to death at San Quentin.

I walked around aimlessly, just thinking about it. Here I was in New York, and my father was going to die on the other side of the continent. In less than five hours.

Then, of course, I realized that it would be eight hours. There's a time difference of three hours between New York and California. He had eight hours to live, and I had eight hours before it was time to mourn him.

How do you wait for a person to die? What do you do, when you know the very minute of death? Do you go to a movie? Watch television, maybe? Read a magazine?

ONE NIGHT OF DEATH

I hadn't even noticed where I was, and I looked up to discover that I'd drifted clear over to Saint Mark's Place. It was natural enough, I used to spend most of my time on that little street, just east of Third Avenue and north of Cooper Square. I used to spend my time with Betty, who used to be my girl.

Before the murder.

Murders change things, you see. They turn things upside down, and suddenly Betty wasn't my girl any more. Suddenly, she wasn't speaking to me any longer. I was a murderer's son.

Dan Bookspan wasn't a murderer's son, though. He was the same rotten, smooth-talking, crooked kind of a bastard as his old man, but his old man was dead now. So Dan Bookspan had my girl.

I got the hell away from Saint Mark's Place. I walked south to an old joint on the corner of Great Jones Street and the Bowery. I sat down on a stool in the back and ordered rye and soda. I sat down there with bums stinking and babbling on either side of me, in a Bowery bar where no one cared that I was just 17 and too young to drink, and I poured the rye in.

The time passed, thank God. The television was going but I didn't look at it, and there were a few brawls but I didn't watch or participate. I just wanted to get loaded and watch the hours go by until it was three in the morning and my father was dead.

I didn't get drunk. I drank slowly, for one thing. More important, I had too much of a fire going inside of me to get tight. I burned the alcohol up before it could get to me, I guess.

By midnight I couldn't stand it any longer. I wanted to be with someone, and being alone was impossible. I couldn't go home, for I knew how important it was to Mom that she be by herself. She had a lot of crying and drinking to do, and I didn't want to get in her way.

There was no one I wanted to see. No one but Betty.

It would have been so good to be with her then, to have her in my arms, holding me close and telling me that everything was going to be all right. What the hell, I thought. I walked over to the phone booth and gave her a ring.

ONE NIGHT STANDS

The phone rang ten times without an answer. If I'd had anything better to do, I'd have given up. But I didn't so I stayed in the booth listening to the phone ring. And after ten rings, she answered it.

She couldn't have been sleeping, for there was a tension in her voice that showed she'd been busy. Her voice was tight and husky.

"Betty," I said "Betty, I want to come over."

There was a pause. "You can't."

"Look, I won't bother you. It's . . . it's a bad night, Betty. I need someone you know? Let me come over."

Again a pause, and a boy's voice in the background. Bookspan's. I gritted my teeth and banged the phone down on the hook. I needed another drink, and I had one. And then I had another, and another.

I left the joint at one, and I walked home. I felt fine, in spite of the liquor I'd had. I walked a straight line and my head was clear as crystal. I tiptoed up the stairs, past the living-room where Mom was drinking and crying.

I found what I was looking for in Dad's bureau drawer. He'd tried to kill Bookspan before you see. Once he bought a gun at a Third Avenue hock-shop, but he never used it, never even pulled its trigger. When he finally shot the bastard, he was in California and the gun was still in the bureau drawer. It was almost as though he had left it there for me.

I left the house as silently as I had entered it, the gun snug and comfortable in my jacket pocket. At one-thirty, I climbed the stairs to the apartment house on Saint Mark's Place.

She didn't let me in, because she didn't have to. They'd left the door open, and I walked in without knocking. I walked through the familiar kitchen to the equally familiar bedroom. I knew that I'd find them there.

I flung open the bedroom door and I saw them lying there, in each other's arms. My girl. My girl, with the guy I hated most in the world. I'd expected it, but it was a hard thing to watch.

Her lips parted for a scream, but she stopped instantly when she saw the gun in my hand. Her face froze in terror, and she looked like

ONE NIGHT OF DEATH

a very little girl just then, a little girl trying to pretend she was a woman.

Bookspan just looked scared. I enjoyed the fear in his eyes, as much as I could have enjoyed anything at the time. I let them look at the gun for several minutes, without saying a word.

Then I told them to close their eyes, and then I walked to the side of the bed and struck each of them on the head with the barrel of the gun. I just used enough force to knock them unconscious. I didn't want to kill them; I couldn't do that.

I tore a bed-sheet into strips of cloth and tied them up. I put their arms tight around each other, tying his hands around her back and her hands around his. Then I gagged them, and I waited.

When they came to, they struggled helplessly while their bodies pressed together. It could have been funny, if the circumstances had been different.

But I didn't laugh. I just watched them for a while, waiting. I put the gun back in my pocket, because I didn't need it any more.

Later, I walked around the apartment, making sure that all the windows were closed tightly. It was precisely three o'clock when I opened all the gas jets full blast and left, shutting the door behind me.

But it was midnight in California.

PACKAGE DEAL

"If I were younger," John Harper said, "I would do this myself. One of the troubles with growing old. Aging makes physical action awkward. A man becomes a planner, an arranger. Responsibility is delegated."

Castle waited.

"If I were younger," Harper went on, "I would kill them myself. I would load a gun and go out after them. I would hunt them down, one after another, and I would shoot them dead. Baron and Milani and Hallander and Ross. I would kill them all."

The old man's mouth spread in a smile.

"A strange picture," he said. "John Harper with blood in his eye. The president of the bank, the past president of Rotary and Kiwanis and the Chamber of Commerce, the leading citizen of Arlington. Going out and killing people. An incongruous picture. Success gets a man, Castle. Removes the spine and intestines. Ties the hands. Success is an incredible surgeon."

"So you hire me."

"So I hire you. Or, to be more precise, we hire you. We've had as much as we can take. We've watched a peaceful, pleasant town taken over by a collection of amateur hoodlums. We've witnessed the inadequacy of a small-town police force faced with big-town operations. We've had enough."

Harper sipped brandy. He was thinking, looking for the right way to phrase what he had to say. "Prostitution," he said suddenly. "And gambling. And protection—storekeepers paying money for the right to remain storekeepers. We've watched four men take control of a town which used to be ours."

Castle nodded. He knew the story already but he wasn't impatient with the old man. He didn't mind getting both the facts and

PACKAGE DEAL

the background behind them. You needed the full picture to do your job properly. He listened.

"I wish we could do it ourselves. Vigilante action, that type of thing. Fortunately, there's also an historical precedent for employing you. Are you familiar with it?"

"The town-tamer," Castle muttered

"The town-tamer. An invention of the American West. The man who cleans up a town for a fee. The man who waives legality when legality must inevitably be abandoned. The man who used a gun instead of a badge when guns are effective and badges are impotent."

"For a fee."

"For a fee," John Harper echoed. "For a fee of ten thousand dollars, in this instance. Ten thousand dollars to rid the world and the town of Arlington of four men. Four malignant men, four little cancers. Baron and Milani and Hallander and Ross."

"Just four?"

"Just four. When the rats die, the mice scatter. Kill four. Kill Lou Baron and Joe Milani and Albert Hallander and Mike Ross. Then the back of the gang will be broken. The rest will run for their lives. The town will breathe clean air again. And the town needs clean air, Mr. Castle, needs it desperately. You may rest assured of that. You are doing more than earning a generous fee. You are performing a service for humanity."

Castle shrugged.

"I'm serious," Harper said. "I know your reputation. You're not a hired killer, sir. You are the twentieth-century version of the town-tamer. I respect you as I could never respect a hired killer. You are performing an important service, sir. I respect you."

Castle lit a cigarette. "The fee," he said.

"Ten thousand dollars. And I'm paying it entirely in advance, Mr. Castle. Because, as I have said, your reputation has preceded you. You'll have no trouble with the local police, but there are always state troopers to contend with. You might wish to leave Arlington in a hurry when the job is finished. As I understand it, the customary method of payment is half in advance and the remaining

133

ONE NIGHT STANDS

half upon completion of the job at hand. I trust you, Mr. Castle. I am paying the full sum in advance. You come well recommended."

Castle took the envelope, slipped it into an inside jacket pocket. It made a bulge there.

"Baron and Milani and Hallander and Ross," the old man said, "four fish. Shoot them in a barrel, Mr. Castle. Shoot them and kill them. They are a disease, a plague."

Castle nodded. "That's all?"

"That is all."

The interview was over. Castle stood up and let Harper show him to the door. He walked quickly to his car and drove off into the night.

Baron and Milani and Hallander and Ross.

Castle had never met them but he knew them all. Small fish, little boys setting up a little town for a little fortune. They were not big men. They didn't have the guts or the brains to play in Chicago or New York or Vegas. They knew their strengths and their limitations. And they cut a nice pie for themselves.

Arlington, Ohio. Population forty-seven thousand. Three small manufacturing concerns, two of them owned by John Harper. One bank, owned by John Harper. Stores and shops, doctors and lawyers. Shop-keepers, workers, professional men, housewives, clerks.

And, for the first time, criminals.

Lou Baron and Joe Milani and Albert Hallander and Mike Ross. And, as a direct result of their presence, a bucketful of hustlers on Lake Street, a handful of horse drops on Main and Limestone, a batch of numbers-runners and a boatload of muscle to make sure everything moved according to plan. Money being drained from Arlington, people being exploited in Arlington, Arlington turning slowly but surely into the private property of four men.

Baron and Milani and Hallander and Ross.

Castle drove to his hotel, went to his room, put ten thousand dollars in his suitcase. He took out a gun, a .45 automatic which could not be traced farther than a St. Louis pawnshop, and slipped

PACKAGE DEAL

the loaded gun into the pocket which had held the ten thousand dollars. The gun made the jacket sag a bit too much and he took out the gun, took off the jacket and strapped on a shoulder holster. The gun fit better this way. With the jacket on, the gun bulged only slightly.

Baron and Milani and Hallander and Ross. Four small fish in a pond too big for them. Ten thousand dollars.

He was ready.

Evening.

A warm night in Arlington. A full moon, no stars, temperature around seventy. Humidity high. Castle walked down Center Street, his car at the hotel, his gun in its holster.

He was working. There were four to be taken and he was taking them in order. Lou Baron was first.

Lou Baron. Short and fat and soft. A beetle from Kansas City, a soft man who had no place in Kerrigan's K.C. mob. A big wheel in Arlington. A man employing women, a pimp on a large scale.

Filth.

Castle waited for Baron. He walked to Lake Street and found a doorway where the shadows eclipsed the moon. And waited.

Baron came out of 137 Lake Street a few minutes after nine. Fat and soft, wearing expensive clothes. Laughing, because they took good care of Baron at 137 Lake Street. They had no choice.

Baron walked alone. Castle waited, waited until the small fat man had passed him on the way to a long black car. Then the gun came out of the holster.

"Baron—"

The little man turned around. Castle's finger tightened on the trigger. There was a loud noise.

The bullet went into Baron's mouth and came out of the back of his head. The bullet had a soft nose and there was a bigger hole on the way out than on the way in. Castle holstered the gun, walked away in the shadows.

ONE NIGHT STANDS

One down.
Three to go.

Milani was easy. Milani lived in a frame house with his wife. That amused Castle, the notion that Milani was a property-owner in Arlington. It was funny.

Milani ran numbers in St. Louis, crossed somebody, pulled out. He was too small to chase. The local people let him alone.

Now people ran numbers for him in Arlington. A change of pace. And Milani's wife, a St. Louis tramp with big breasts and no brains, helped Milani spend his money that stupid people bet on three-digit numbers.

Milani was easy. He was home and the door was locked. Castle rang the bell. And Milani, safe and secure and self-important, did not bother with peepholes. He opened the door.

And caught a .45-caliber bullet over the heart.

Two down and two to go.

Hallander was a gun man. Castle didn't know much about him, just a few rumbles that made their way over the coast-to-coast grapevine. Little things.

A gun, a torpedo, a zombie. A bodyguard out of Chi who goofed too many times. A killer who loved to kill, a little man with dead eyes who was nude without a gun. A psychopath. So many killers were psychopaths. Castle hated them with the hatred of the businessmen for the competitive hobbyist. Killing Baron and Milani had been on the order of squashing cockroaches under the heel of a heavy shoe. Killing Hallander was a pleasure.

Hallander did not live in a house like Milani or go to women like Baron. Hallander had no use for women, only for a gun. He lived alone in a small apartment on the outskirts of town. His car, four years old, was parked in his garage. He could have afforded a better car. But to Hallander, money was not to be spent. It was chips in a poker game. He held onto his chips.

PACKAGE DEAL

He was well protected—a doorman screened visitors, an elevator operator knew whom he took upstairs. But Hallander made no friends. Five dollars quieted the doorman forever. Five dollars sealed the lips of the elevator operator.

Castle knocked on Hallander's door.

A peephole opened. A peephole closed. Hallander drew a gun and fired through the door.

And missed.

Castle shot the lock off, kicked the door open. Hallander missed again.

And died.

With a bullet in the throat.

The elevator operator took Castle back to the first floor. The doorman passed him through to the street. He got into his car, turned the key in the ignition, drove back to the center of Arlington.

Three down.

Just one more.

"We can deal," Mike Ross said. "You got your money. You hit three out of four. You can leave me be."

- Castle said nothing. They were alone, he and Ross. The brains of the Arlington enterprise sat in an easy chair with a slow smile on his face. He knew about Baron and Milani and Hallander.

"You did a job already," Ross said. "You got paid already. You want money? Fifteen thousand. Cash. Then you disappear."

Castle shook his head.

"Why not? Hot-shot Harper won't sue you. You'll have his ten grand and fifteen of mine and you'll disappear. Period. No trouble, no sweat, no nothing. Nobody after you looking to even things up. Tell you the truth, I'm glad to see the three of them out of the way. More for me and no morons getting in the way. I'm glad you took them. Just so you don't take me."

"I've got a job to do."

137

ONE NIGHT STANDS

"Twenty grand. Thirty. What's a man's life worth? Name your price, Castle. Name it!"

"No price."

Mike Ross laughed. "Everybody has a price. Everybody. You aren't that special. I can buy you, Castle."

Ross bought death. He bought one bullet and death came at once. He fell on his face and died. Castle wiped off the gun, flipped it onto the floor. He had taken chances, using the same gun four times. But the four times had taken less than one night. Morning had not come yet. The Arlington police force still slept.

He dropped the gun to the floor and got out of there.

A phone rang in Chicago. A man lifted it, held it to his ear.

"Castle," a voice said.

"Job done?"

"All done."

"How many hits?"

"Four of them," Castle said. "Four off the top."

"Give me the picture."

"The machinery is there with nobody to run it," Castle said. "The town is lonely."

The man chuckled. "You're good," he said. "You're very good. We'll be down tomorrow."

"Come on in," Castle said. "The water's fine."

PROFESSIONAL KILLER

He was sitting alone in a hotel room.

He was, possibly, the most average man in the world. His clothes were carefully chosen to pass in a crowd—dull brown oxfords, a brown gabardine suit, a white shirt and a slim brown tie. On his head he usually wore an almost shapeless brown felt hat, but the hat now rested on a chair in a corner of the room. He was neither short nor fat nor tall nor thin.

Even his face was uninteresting. His features were unimpressive in themselves, and they didn't add up to a distinctive face. He had the usual number of noses, eyes, mouths, and so on—but somehow each feature seemed to be lifted from another dull face, so that he himself possessed no facial character whatsoever.

In many professions such a lack of individuality would be a handicap. A salesman without a face has a difficult time making a living. An executive, a merchant—almost anyone has a better chance of success if people remember his face and take notice of him. But the man in the hotel room was very pleased with his nondescript appearance, and did what he could to make himself even less noticeable. In his business it was an asset—perhaps the most important asset he possessed.

The man in the hotel room was named Harry Varden. He lived with his wife in a small house in Mamaroneck, in lower Westchester County. He had no children and no close friends.

He was a professional killer.

His office was a hotel room, and the location of this particular hotel room is of little importance. His office changed every week, and when he moved from one hotel to another, his phone number was placed in the classified section of the *New York Times*. A customer could always find him.

ONE NIGHT STANDS

He was reading. He read a good deal, since there was nothing else to do while he waited for the phone to ring. Most days he spent morning and afternoon reading, and most afternoons and mornings were quite barren of phone calls. At $5000 a killing, he didn't need too large a volume of business.

This afternoon, however, the phone rang.

He closed his book, walked to the edge of the bed, sat down and lifted the receiver. "Hello," he said, in a voice that was as unimpressive as his appearance.

"Hello." The voice on the other end of the line was a woman's. He waited.

"I . . ." the woman began. "Who is this?"

"Whom do you want?"

The woman hesitated. "Are . . . are you the man?"

Harry Varden sighed to himself. He despised the hesitation and ineptness on the part of some clients, the clients who wouldn't open their mouths, the ones who were so terribly unsure of themselves. Professionals were different. Some of his clients, the ones who used him three or four times a year, had no trouble coming to the point at once.

"What man do you want?" he asked.

"The man who . . . the man with the number in the paper."

Coward, he thought. *Come on and speak your peace*. And aloud he said, "Yes, I'm the man."

"Will you do a job for me?"

Suddenly he was angry. The fee became of little importance now; his whole mind was set on forcing this woman to talk, on opening her up and making her say the words she didn't want to say.

"Don't be coy," he snapped. "What the hell do you want?"

After a long pause, the woman said, "I want you to murder my husband."

"Why?"

"I . . . what do you mean?"

PROFESSIONAL KILLER

"Look," he said, tiredly, "you want me to kill your husband. I want to know why."

"But I thought I just told you what you should do and sent you the money and that was all. I mean . . ."

"I don't care what you thought. You can open up or find another boy."

And he hung up.

He waited for the phone to ring again, knowing for certain that it would ring and that this time she would talk. It occurred to him that this was the first time he had acted in such a manner, the first time he had even pretended to care any more about a job than the name and the location of the victim. But there was some familiar whine in the woman's voice, some peculiar nagging quality that made him think he had heard it before. For some reason he disliked the owner of the voice intensely.

The phone rang, and the woman said at once, "I'm sorry. I don't understand."

"Okay. Give me the story."

She paused for a second and began. "I don't love my husband," she said. "I don't think I ever really loved him, and now there's somebody else, if you know what I mean. That is, I've met this other man and he and I are in love with each other, so naturally . . ."

Once she got started she didn't seem able to stop. Harry Varden listened half-heartedly, wondering why in the name of the Lord he had started her going. He couldn't care less why he was earning his $5000 (which by this time only a strict sense of professionalism kept him from raising to $7500) and he cared even less about the woman's married life.

But she kept right on. Her husband was dull and boring. He never talked to her, never paid any attention to her, never told her what was on his mind. She didn't even know for certain where he worked or what he did for a living.

Oh, he was a good provider, but there were more important things in a woman's life. She needed to feel that she was an important and

141

distinctive woman with an equally important and distinctive man to love her. And her husband was dull and not the least bit important or distinctive or at all interesting, and ...

The voice was one he had heard a million times in the past. For a moment it seemed that he had indeed heard this same voice before, but he decided that it was only the routine nature of the sentiments expressed which made the voice seem familiar.

Besides, Harry Varden never remembered a voice and rarely recalled a face. He himself was neither noticed nor remembered, and he retaliated unconsciously by means of a poor memory.

And she had met a man, a dashing, romantic man who sold brushes from door to door, and if her husband were dead she would have all his money, because he did seem to have a great deal of money although she wasn't quite sure how he came by it, and with the money she could marry the brush salesman, and they could live happily, albeit not forever, and besides there was the insurance if he had insurance and she supposed again that he did although again she wasn't sure, and for all she knew he *sold* insurance, but at any rate for all these reasons she wanted to pay Harry Varden $5000, in return for which payment he was to shoot her husband in his own home, some evening at eight o'clock or thereabouts, at which time she would be home and would be most willing to swear that Harry Varden was not the murderer, in the event that Harry Varden was ever caught, which was improbable from what she had heard.

By the time she had finished, Harry Varden was almost as tired as she was. The woman was a colossal bore, and he felt a considerable amount of sympathy for her uninteresting and opaque husband. He could easily understand why such a man didn't spend much time talking to such a woman.

In fact he felt that it was a shame he had to shoot the man, with whom he felt some sympathy, rather than the woman, whom it would be a genuine pleasure to shoot. But business, sadly, was business.

"I'll want the money in advance, of course," he said.

PROFESSIONAL KILLER

"I see," she said. "But why does the money have to be in advance?"

"That's the way I do business."

"I see. But then . . . I mean, you could just take the money and then never do the job for me, I mean . . ."

And, of course, he hung up for the second time.

When he answered the phone the third time she began talking quickly even before he had time to put the receiver to his ear, saying that she was very sorry and would he please forgive her since of course he was honest and she should have known better to say such a thing, or even to think such a thing, but $5000 was a large sum of money, wasn't it?

He agreed that it was.

"Look," he said, tiring of the game, "I want you to put $5000 in tens and twenties in a bag or something. Lock it in a Grand Central locker and mail the key to PO Box 412. In the envelope with the key put the time you want the job done, the name of the party and the address. Get that key in the mail today and the job will be done tomorrow night. Okay?"

"I guess so."

"You got the box number?"

"Box 412," she said.

"Excellent," he murmured, and he replaced the receiver on the cradle. He waited for a moment, wondering whether she might call back for some strange reason. Then, after a moment had passed without the phone ringing, he picked up his book and began reading once again.

It took him a moment to recapture the line of thought in the book, but he re-read a paragraph and immersed himself once again in the text and read for the remainder of the afternoon without interruption.

The following day was routine. Lesser men than Harry Varden might have considered it a rut, but he was content with his lot. Out of the "office" at five, a quick walk to Grand Central, the 5:17 to Mamaroneck, a slightly longer walk to his home, dinner, and a good

ONE NIGHT STANDS

book in his hands while Mary washed the dishes and turned on the television set.

It was a good life—well-ordered, intelligently planned, more money in the bank than either he or Mary could ever spend, and all the comforts that anyone could want in a home.

When he bedded down for the night at a few minutes after eleven, he went to sleep easily. There was a time, long ago when he was new in the trade, when sleeping had been a problem. Time, however, healed all wounds, and routine removed whatever scruples might once have been involved in his profession.

He did his job, and when his job was done he slept. It was simple enough, certainly nothing to lose any sleep over.

In fact, it was a rare occasion when he took any interest in his work greater than the interest in doing a clean and workmanlike job. Today, for example, he had become far too involved with that woman. A client should never even begin to become a person. A client should be no more than a voice on a telephone, just as a victim should be merely a name scrawled (more often, for some obscure reason, type-written or hand printed) on a piece of paper. When either became a real person, the job became several times as difficult.

An ideal job was totally impersonal. It was much easier to erase a scrap of paper than to obliterate a human life. One time he had followed a potential victim long enough to gain some insight into the other's personality. It was infinitely more difficult to pull the trigger, and he had almost bunged that particular job.

For one moment he found himself almost dreading tomorrow's job, almost hoping that the money would not be at the locker, that the key would not arrive at his post office box.

Then he told himself that he was being foolish, and a moment later he was asleep.

His breakfast, on the table when he descended the staircase in the morning, was the same breakfast he'd eaten for a good many years—orange juice, cinnamon toast, and black coffee. As usual, he was out the door by 7:53 and on the 8:02 to Grand Central. He permitted

PROFESSIONAL KILLER

himself the luxury of a taxi to the Post Office, leaning back in the back seat of the cab and enjoying the first cigarette of the day.

He studied the cab-driver's face in the mirror, wondering idly whether he had taken this cab before, whether he had met this very driver somewhere else. At times his lack of a memory for people disturbed him; at other times, he recognized it as a double blessing.

For one thing, if his memory were good he would be constantly hailing people whom he had met and who, since he himself was so inconspicuous, would not remember him at all.

And, of course, there was the matter of conscience. While he didn't consciously feel any remorse over a murder, he was intelligent enough to realize that he was unconsciously beset with periodic visitations of guilt.

When the faces and voices of clients and victims were reduced by time to a vague blur, the guilt was diminished through his own removal from a vivid recollection of the entire affair.

The envelope was in his box. He removed it, closed the box, and took another cab back to Grand Central. He removed the key from the envelope without troubling to glance at the slip of paper, only noticing that the name and address were type-written.

He located the locker, opened it, and removed $5000 which he pocketed at once. Then he took a room at another hotel in the area.

Once in the hotel, his whole mind and body slipped into the role of the killer, the comfortable and familiar role of the hired murderer.

He had become a machine. The money was in his pocket; in a short while it would be in his bank account. He would now have to purchase a fresh gun from the pawnbroker on Third Avenue, pick up a silencer for the gun, place an ad in the *Times* announcing the change of address, and prepare himself for the job.

The gun cost him $100. The silencer, purchased in another pawnshop a block further down Third Avenue, set him back another $25. The ad, which stated simply that Acme Services was located at 758 Grosvenor, cost very little. The ad meant, of course, that Harry Varden was now in room 758 at the Grosvenor. To avoid any con-

ONE NIGHT STANDS

fusion it was placed in the SITUATIONS WANTED, MALE column —the clients knew where to look.

The next stop was the bank. The money was deposited to his account, quickly and easily. He walked out with a gun in his shoulder holster, a silencer in an inside jacket pocket, a slip of paper still in the envelope in his pants pocket, and the brown felt hat riding easily on his head. He was walking on familiar ground.

The attack of nerves which the book said was inevitable at such a moment was entirely absent, and this worried him at times. Perhaps he ought to feel more. Perhaps the work should revolt him. But it didn't, and he resolved that this was really something to be thankful for. Perhaps that was the secret of Harry Varden's happiness; he invariably managed to mentally convert every apparent liability into an asset.

He ate lunch before opening the envelope once again. He did this on purpose; experience had taught him that the longer he waited before learning even the victim's name, the easier the whole process became.

Lunch finished, he returned to the hotel room, sat down on the bed, and pulled the envelope from his pocket. He opened it, pulled out the small slip of paper, and unfolded the slip methodically.

For a moment he was angry. For a moment the anger burned in him like a blue flame, but this was only for a moment, and the emotion passed quite rapidly. With it, the thought of a possible course of action vanished from his mind. He remembered the old maxim about a lawyer who tried his own case having a fool for a client.

He picked up the receiver and asked for a number. When the phone was answered a soft voice said "Hello" in a guarded fashion.

"Pete?" he said. "This is Harry. Look, I've a job for you—more work than I can handle. It's got to be tonight. Okay?"

"Right."

PROFESSIONAL KILLER

He smiled to himself. "Tonight at 8," he said. "The mark's a woman living at 43 Riverton, in Mamaroneck. It's exactly eight minutes' walking time from the railroad station."

PSEUDO IDENTITY

Somewhere between four and four-thirty, Howard Jordan called his wife. "It looks like another late night," he told her. "The spot TV copy for Prentiss was full of holes. I'll be here half the night rewriting it."

"You'll stay in town?"

"No choice."

"I hope you won't have trouble finding a room."

"I'll make reservations now. Or there's always the office couch."

"Well," Carolyn said, and he heard her sigh the sigh designed to reassure him that she was sorry he would not be coming home, "I'll see you tomorrow night, then. Don't forget to call the hotel."

"I won't."

He did not call the hotel. At five, the office emptied out. At five minutes after five, Howard Jordan cleared off his desk, packed up his attache case and left the building. He had a steak in a small restaurant around the corner from his office, then caught a cab south and west to a four-story red brick building on Christopher Street. His key opened the door, and he walked in.

In the hallway, a thin girl with long blonde hair smiled at him. "Hi, Roy."

"Hello, baby."

"Too much," she said, eyeing his clothes. "The picture of middle-class respectability."

"A mere facade. A con perpetrated upon the soulless bosses."

"Crazy. There's a party over at Ted and Betty's. You going?"

"I might."

"See you there."

He entered his own apartment, tucked his attache case behind a low bookcase improvised of bricks and planks. In the small closet he

PSEUDO IDENTITY

hung his gray sharkskin suit, his button-down shirt, his rep-striped tie. He dressed again in tight Levi's and a bulky brown turtleneck sweater, changed his black moccasin toe oxfords for white hole-in-the-toe tennis sneakers. He left his wallet in the pocket of the sharkskin suit and pocketed another wallet, this one containing considerably less cash, no credit cards and a few cards identifying him as Roy Baker.

He spent an hour playing chess in the back room of a Sullivan Street coffee house, winning two games of three. He joined friends in a bar a few blocks away and got into an overly impassioned argument on the cultural implications of Camp; when the bartender ejected them, he took his friends along to the party in the East Village apartment of Ted Marsh and Betty Haniford. Someone had brought a guitar, and he sat on the floor drinking wine and listening to the singing.

Ginny, the long-haired blonde who had an apartment in his building, drank too much wine. He walked her home, and the night air sobered her.

"Come up for a minute or two," she said. "I want you to hear what my analyst said this afternoon. I'll make us some coffee."

"Groovy," he said, and went upstairs with her. He enjoyed the conversation and the coffee and Ginny. An hour later, around one thirty, he returned to his own apartment and went to sleep.

In the morning he rose, showered, put on a fresh white shirt, another striped tie, and the same gray sharkskin suit, and rode uptown to his office.

It had begun innocently enough. From the time he'd made the big jump from senior copywriter at Lowell, Burham & Plescow to copy chief at Keith Wenrall Associates, he had found himself working late more and more frequently. While the late hours never bothered him, merely depriving him of the company of a whining wife, the midnight train to New Hope was a constant source of aggravation. He never got to bed before two-thirty those nights he rode it, and then had to

ONE NIGHT STANDS

drag himself out of bed just four and a half hours later in order to be at his desk by nine.

It wasn't long before he abandoned the train and spent those late nights in a midtown hotel. This proved an imperfect solution, substituting inconvenience and expense for sleeplessness. It was often difficult to find a room at a late hour, always impossible to locate one for less than twelve dollars; and hotel rooms, however well appointed, did not provide such amenities as a toothbrush or a razor, not to mention a change of underwear and a clean shirt. Then too, there was something disturbingly temporary and marginal about a hotel room. It felt even less like home than did his split-level miasma in Bucks County.

An apartment, he realized, would overcome all of these objections while actually saving him money. He could rent a perfectly satisfactory place for a hundred dollars a month, less than he presently spent on hotels, and it would always be there for him, with fresh clothing in the closet and a razor and toothbrush in the bathroom.

He found the listing in the classified pages—*Christopher St, 1 rm, bth, ktte, frnshd, util, $90 mth*. He translated this and decided that a one-room apartment on Christopher Street with bathroom and kitchenette, furnished, with utilities included at ninety dollars per month, was just what he was looking for. He called the landlord and asked when he could see the apartment.

"Come around after dinner," the landlord said. He gave him the address and asked his name.

"Baker," Howard Jordan said. "Roy Baker."

After he hung up he tried to imagine why he had given a false name. It was a handy device when one wanted to avoid being called back, but it did seem pointless in this instance. Well, no matter, he decided. He would make certain the landlord got his name straight when he rented the apartment. Meanwhile, he had problems enough changing a junior copywriter's flights of literary fancy into something

PSEUDO IDENTITY

that might actually convince a man that the girls would love him more if he used the client's brand of gunk on his hair.

The landlord, a birdlike little man with thick metal-rimmed glasses, was waiting for Jordan. He said, "Mr. Baker? Right this way. First floor in the rear. Real nice."

The apartment was small but satisfactory. When he agreed to rent it the landlord produced a lease, and Jordan immediately changed his mind about clearing up the matter of his own identity. A lease, he knew, would be infinitely easier to break without his name on it. He gave the document a casual reading, then signed it "Roy Baker" in a handwriting quite unlike his own.

"Now I'll want a hundred and eighty dollars," the landlord said. "That's a month's rent in advance and a month's security."

Jordan reached for his checkbook, then realized his bank would be quite unlikely to honor a check with Roy Baker's signature on it. He paid the landlord in cash, and arranged to move in the next day. He spent the following day's lunch hour buying extra clothing for the apartment, selecting bed linen, and finally purchasing a suitcase to accommodate the items he had bought. On a whim, he had the suitcase monogrammed "R.B." That night he worked late, told Carolyn he would be staying in a hotel, then carried the suitcase to his apartment, put his new clothes in the closet, put his new toothbrush and razor in the tiny bathroom and, finally, made his bed and lay in it. At this point Roy Baker was no more than a signature on a lease and two initials on a suitcase.

Two months later, Roy Baker was a person.

The process by which Roy Baker's bones were clad with flesh was a gradual one. Looking back on it, Jordan could not tell exactly how it had begun, or at what point it had become purposeful. Baker's personal wardrobe came into being when Jordan began to make the rounds of Village bars and coffeehouses, and wanted to look more like a neighborhood resident and less like a celebrant from uptown. He bought denim trousers, canvas shoes, bulky sweaters; and when

ONE NIGHT STANDS

he shed his three-button suit and donned his Roy Baker costume, he was transformed as utterly as Bruce Wayne clad in Batman's mask and cape.

When he met people in the building or around the neighborhood, he automatically introduced himself as Baker. This was simply expedient; it wouldn't do to get into involved discussions with casual acquaintances, telling them that he answered to one name but lived under another, but by being Baker instead of Jordan, he could play a far more interesting role. Jordan, after all, was a square, a Madison Avenue copy chief, an animal of little interest to the folksingers and artists and actors he met in the Village. Baker, on the other hand, could be whatever Jordan wanted him to be. Before long his identity took form: he was an artist, he'd been unable to do any serious work since his wife's tragic death, and for the time being he was stuck in a square job uptown with a commercial art studio.

This identity he had picked for Baker was a source of occasional amusement to him. Its expedience aside, he was not blind to its psychological implications. Substitute *writer* for *artist* and one approached his own situation. He had long dreamed of being a writer, but had made no efforts toward serious writing since his marriage to Carolyn. The bit about the tragic death of his wife was nothing more than simple wish-fulfillment. Nothing would have pleased him more than Carolyn's death, so he had incorporated this dream in Baker's biography.

As the weeks passed, Baker accumulated more and more of the trappings of personality. He opened a bank account. It was, after all, inconvenient to pay the rent in cash. He joined a book club and promptly wound up on half the world's mailing lists. He got a letter from his congressman advising him of latest developments in Washington and the heroic job his elected representative was doing to safeguard his interests. Before very long, he found himself heading for his Christopher Street apartment even on nights when he did not have to work late at all.

PSEUDO IDENTITY

Interestingly enough, his late work actually decreased once he was settled in the apartment. Perhaps he had only developed the need to work late out of a larger need to avoid going home to Carolyn. In any event, now that he had a place to go after work, he found it far less essential to stay around the office after five o'clock. He rarely worked late more than one night a week—but he always spent three nights a week in town, and often four.

Sometimes he spent the evening with friends. Sometimes he stayed in his apartment and rejoiced in the blessings of solitude. Other times he combined the best of two worlds by finding an agreeable Village female to share his solitude.

He kept waiting for the double life to catch up with him, anticipating the tension and insecurity which were always a component of such living patterns in the movies and on television. He expected to be discovered, or overcome by guilt, or otherwise to have the error of his dual ways brought forcibly home to him. But this did not happen. His office work showed a noticeable improvement; he was not only more efficient, but his copy was fresher, more inspired, more creative. He was doing more work in less time and doing a better job of it. Even his home life improved, if only in that there was less of it.

Divorce? He thought about it, imagined the joy of being Roy Baker on a full-time basis. It would be financially devastating, he knew. Carolyn would wind up with the house and the car and the lion's share of his salary, but Roy Baker could survive on a mere fraction of Howard Jordan's salary, existing quite comfortably without house or car. He never relinquished the idea of asking Carolyn for a divorce, nor did he ever quite get around to it—until one night he saw her leaving a night club on West Third Street, her black hair blowing in the wind, her step drunkenly unsteady, and a man's arm curled possessively around her waist.

His first reaction was one of astonishment that anyone would actually desire her. With all the vibrant, fresh-bodied girls in the Village, why would anyone be interested in Carolyn? It made no sense to him.

ONE NIGHT STANDS

Then, suddenly, his puzzlement gave way to absolute fury. She had been cold to him for years, and now she was running around with other men, adding insult to injury. She let him support her, let him pay off the endless mortgage on the horrible house, let him sponsor her charge accounts while she spent her way toward the list of Ten Best-Dressed Women. She took everything from him and gave nothing to him, and all the while she was giving it to someone else.

He knew, then, that he hated her, that he had always hated her and, finally, that he was going to do something about it.

What? Hire detectives? Gather evidence? Divorce her as an adulteress? Small revenge, hardly the punishment that fit the crime. No. No, *he* could not possibly do anything about it. It would be too much out of character for him to take positive action. He was the good clean-living, midtown-square type, good old Howie Jordan. He would do all that such a man could do, bearing his new knowledge in silence, pretending that he knew nothing, and going on as before.

But Roy Baker could do more.

From that day on he let his two lives overlap. On the nights when he stayed in town he went directly from the office to a nearby hotel, took a room, rumpled up the bed so that it would look as though it had been slept in, then left the hotel by back staircase and rear exit. After a quick cab ride downtown and a change of clothes, he became Roy Baker again and lived Roy Baker's usual life, spending just a little more time than usual around West Third Street. It wasn't long before he saw her again. This time he followed her. He found out that her lover was a self-styled folksinger named Stud Clement, and he learned by discreet inquiries that Carolyn was paying Stud's rent.

"Stud inherited her from Phillie Wells when Phillie split for the Coast," someone told him. "She's got some square husband in Connecticut or someplace. If Stud's not on the scene, she don't care who she goes home with." She had been at this, then, for some time. He smiled bitterly. It was true, he decided; the husband was really the last to know.

PSEUDO IDENTITY

He went on using the midtown hotel, creating a careful pattern for his life, and he kept careful patterns on Stud Clement. One night when Carolyn didn't come to town, he managed to stand next to the big folksinger in a Hudson Street bar and listen to him talk. He caught the slight Tennessee accent, the pitch of the voice, the type of words that Clement used.

Through it all he waited for his hatred to die, waited for his fury to cool. In a sense she had done no more to him than he had done to her. He half-expected that he would lose his hatred sooner or later, but he found that he hated her more every day, not only for cheating but for making him an ad man instead of a writer, for making him live in that house instead of a Village apartment, for all the things she had done to ruin every aspect of his life. If it had not been for her, he would have been Roy Baker all his life. She had made a Howard Jordan of him, and for that he would hate her forever.

Once he realized this, he made the phone call. "I gotta see you tonight," he said.

"Stud?"

So the imitation was successful. "Not at my place," he said quickly. "193 Christopher, Apartment 1-D. Seven-thirty, no sooner and no later. And don't be going near my place."

"Trouble?"

"Just be there," he said, and hung up.

His own phone rang in less than five minutes. He smiled a bitter smile as he answered it.

She said, "Howard? I was wondering, you're not coming home tonight, are you? You'll have to stay at your hotel in town?"

"I don't know," he said. "I've got a lot of work, but I hate to be away from you so much. Maybe I'll let it slide for a night—"

"No!" He heard her gasp. Then she recovered, and her voice was calm when she spoke again, "I mean, your career comes first, darling. You know that. You shouldn't think of me. Think of your job."

"Well," he said, enjoying all this, "I'm not sure—"

155

ONE NIGHT STANDS

"I've got a dreary headache anyway, darling. Why not stay in town? We'll have the weekend together—"

He let her talk him into it. After she rang off, he called his usual hotel and made his usual reservation for eleven-thirty. He went back to work, left the office at five-thirty, signed the register downstairs and left the building. He had a quick bite at a lunch counter and was back at his desk at six o'clock, after signing the book again on the way in.

At a quarter to seven he left the building again, this time failing to sign himself out. He took a cab to his apartment and was inside it by ten minutes after seven. At precisely seven-thirty there was a knock on his door. He answered it, and she stared at him as he dragged her inside. She couldn't figure it out; her face contorted.

"I'm going to kill you, Carolyn," he said, and showed her the knife. She died slowly, and noisily. Her cries would have brought out the National Guard anywhere else in the country, but they were in New York now, and New Yorkers never concern themselves with the shrieks of dying women.

He took the few clothes that did not belong to Baker, scooped up Carolyn's purse, and got out of the apartment. From a pay phone on Sheridan Square he called the air terminal and made a reservation. Then he taxied back to the office and slipped inside, again without writing his name in the register.

At eleven-fifteen he left the office, went to his hotel and slept much more soundly than he had expected. He went to the office in the morning and had his secretary put in three calls to New Hope. No one answered.

That was Friday. He took his usual train home, rang his bell a few times, used his key, called Carolyn's name several times, then made himself a drink. After half an hour he called the next door neighbor and asked her if she knew where his wife was. She didn't. After another three hours he called the police.

Sunday a local policeman came around to see him. Evidently Carolyn had had her fingerprints taken once, maybe when she'd held

PSEUDO IDENTITY

a civil service job before they were married. The New York police had found the body Saturday evening, and it had taken them a little less than twenty-four hours to run a check on the prints and trace Carolyn to New Hope.

"I hoped I wouldn't have to tell you this," the policeman said. "When you reported your wife missing, we talked to some of the neighbors. It looks as though she was—uh— stepping out on you, Mr. Jordan. I'm afraid it had been going on for some time. There were men she met in New York. Does the name Roy Baker mean anything to you?"

"No. Was he—"

"I'm afraid he was one of the men she was seeing, Mr. Jordan. I'm afraid he killed her, sir."

Howard's reactions combined hurt and loss and bewilderment in proper proportion. He almost broke down when they had him view the body but managed to hold himself together stoically. He learned from the New York police that Roy Baker was a Village type, evidently some sort of irresponsible artist. Baker had made a reservation on a plane shortly after killing Carolyn but hadn't picked up his ticket, evidently realizing that the police would be able to trace him. He'd no doubt take a plane under another name, but they were certain they would catch up with him before too long.

"He cleared out in a rush," the policeman said. "Left his clothes, never got to empty out his bank account. A guy like this, he's going to turn up in a certain kind of place. The Village, North Beach in Frisco, maybe New Orleans. He'll be back in the Village within a year, I'll bet on it, and when he does we'll pick him up."

For form's sake, the New York police checked Jordan's whereabouts at the time of the murder, and they found that he'd been at his office until eleven-fifteen, except for a half hour when he'd had a sandwich around the corner, and that he had spent the rest of the night at the hotel where he always stayed when he worked late.

That, incredibly, was all there was to it.

ONE NIGHT STANDS

After a suitable interval, Howard put the New Hope house on the market and sold it almost immediately at a better price than he had thought possible. He moved to town, stayed at his alibi hotel while he checked the papers for a Village apartment.

He was in a cab, heading downtown for a look at a three-room apartment on Horatio Street, before he realized suddenly that he could not possibly live in the Village, not now. He was known there as Roy Baker, and if he went there he would be identified as Roy Baker and arrested as Roy Baker, and that would be the end of it.

"Better turn around," he told the cab driver. "Take me back to the hotel. I changed my mind."

He spent another two weeks in the hotel, trying to think things through, looking for a safe way to live Roy Baker's life again. If there was an answer, he couldn't find it. The casual life of the Village had to stay out of bounds.

He took an apartment uptown on the East Side. It was quite expensive but he found it cold and charmless. He took to spending his free evenings at midtown nightclubs, where he drank a little too much and spent a great deal of money to see poor floor shows. He didn't get out often, though, because he seemed to be working late more frequently now. It was harder and harder to get everything done on time. On top of that, his work had lost its sharpness; he had to go over blocks of copy again and again to get them right.

Revelation came slowly, painfully. He began to see just what he had done to himself.

In Roy Baker, he had found the one perfect life for himself. The Christopher Street apartment, the false identity, the new world of new friends and different clothes and words and customs, had been a world he took to with ease because it was the perfect world for him. The mechanics of preserving this dual identity, the taut fabric of lies that clothed it, the childlike delight in pure secrecy, had added a sharp element of excitement to it all. He had enjoyed being Roy Baker; more, he had enjoyed being Howard Jordan playing at being Roy

PSEUDO IDENTITY

Baker. The double life suited him so perfectly that he had felt no great need to divorce Carolyn.

Instead, he had killed her—and killed Roy Baker in the bargain, erased him very neatly, put him out of the picture for all time.

Howard bought a pair of Levi's, a turtleneck sweater, a pair of white tennis sneakers. He kept these clothes in the closet of his Sutton Place apartment, and now and then when he spent a solitary evening there he dressed in his Roy Baker costume and sat on the floor drinking California wine straight from the jug. He wished he were playing chess in the back room of a coffee house, or arguing art and religion in a Village bar, or listening to a blue guitar at a loft party.

He could dress up all he wanted in his Roy Baker costume, but it wouldn't work. He could drink wine and play guitar music on his stereo, but that wouldn't work, either. He could buy women, but he couldn't walk them home from Village parties and make love to them in third-floor walk-ups.

He had to be Howard Jordan.

Carolyn or no Carolyn, married or single, New Hope split-level or Sutton Place apartment, one central fact remained unchanged. He simply did not like being Howard Jordan.

RIDE A WHITE HORSE

Andy Hart stared unbelievingly at the door of Whitey's Tavern. The door was closed and padlocked, and the bar was unlighted. He checked his watch and noted that it was almost 7:30. Whitey should have opened hours ago.

Andy turned and strode to the candy store on the corner. He was a small man, but his rapid walk made up for his short legs. He walked as he did everything else—precisely, with no waste motion.

Hey," he asked the man behind the counter, "how come Whitey didn't open up yet?"

"He's closed down for the next two weeks. Got caught serving minors." Andy thanked him and left.

The news was disturbing. It didn't annoy him tremendously, but it did break up a long-established routine. Ever since he had started working as a book-keeper at Murrow's Department Store, eleven years ago, he had been in the habit of eating a solitary meal at the Five Star Diner and drinking a few beers at Whitey's. He had just finished dinner, and now he found himself with no place to go.

Standing on the streetcorner, staring at the front of the empty bar, he had a vague sensation that he was missing something. Here he was, 37 years old, and there was nowhere in the city for him to go. He had no family, and his only friends were his drinking companions at Whitey's. He could go back to his room, but there he would have only the four walls for company. He momentarily envied the married men who worked in his department. It might be nice to have a wife and kids to come home to.

The thought passed as quickly as it had come. After all, there was no reason to be broken-hearted over a closed bar. There was undoubtedly another bar in the neighborhood where the beer was as

RIDE A WHITE HORSE

good and the people as friendly. He glanced around and noticed a bar directly across the street.

There was a large neon sign over the doorway, with the outline of a horse and the words "White Horse Cafe." The door was a bright red, and music from a juke box wafted through it.

Andy hesitated. There was a bar, all right. He had passed it many times in the past, but had never thought to enter it. It seemed a little flashy to him, a little bit too high-tone. But tonight, he decided, he'd see how it was on the inside. A change of pace wouldn't hurt him at all.

He crossed the street and entered. A half-dozen men were seated at the bar, and several couples occupied booths on the side. The juke box was playing a song which he had heard before, but he couldn't remember the title. He walked to the rear, hung his coat on a peg, and took the end seat.

He ordered a beer and sat nursing it. He studied his reflection in the mirror. His looks were average—neatly-combed brown hair, brown eyes, and a prominent chin. His smile was pleasant, but he didn't smile too often. He was, all in all, a pretty average guy.

The time passed slowly. Andy finished his beer and ordered another, and then another. Some of the people left the bar and others entered, but he saw no one he recognized. He was beginning to regret coming to the White Horse. The beer was fine and the music was nice enough, but he had no more company than the four walls of his room provided.

Then, while he was drinking his fourth beer, the door opened and she entered. He saw her at once. He had glanced to the door every time it opened in the hope of seeing an acquaintance, and each time he had turned back to his glass. This time, however, he couldn't turn his eyes away from her.

She was tall, very pretty, with long blond hair that fell to her shoulders. She took off her coat and hung it up and Andy could see that she was more than just pretty. Her skirt clung to her hips and hugged her thighs, and her breasts threatened to break through the

ONE NIGHT STANDS

tight film of her sweater. Andy couldn't stop looking at her. He knew that he was staring, but he couldn't help himself. She was the most beautiful woman he had ever seen.

He was surprised when she walked over and sat down on the stool beside him. Actually, it was natural enough. There were only two other empty stools at the bar. But to Andy it seemed like the rarest of coincidences.

He was glad that she was sitting next to him but at the same time he was embarrassed. He felt a desire for her which was stronger than anything he had experienced in years. He had neither needed nor wanted a woman in a long while, but now he felt an instantaneous physical craving for her.

The girl ordered a sidecar and sipped at it, and Andy forced himself to drink his beer. He wanted desperately to start a conversation with her but couldn't think of a way to begin. He waited, listening to the music, until she finished her drink.

"Miss," he said nervously, "could I buy you another?"

She turned and looked at him for a long moment, and he felt himself flush. "Yes," she said at last. "Thank you."

He ordered a sidecar for her and another beer for himself, and they began talking. He was amazed to discover that he was able to talk freely and easily to her, and that she in turn seemed interested in everything that he had to say. He had wanted to talk to anybody in the world, and talking to her was almost the answer to a prayer.

He told her everything about himself—his name, his job, and the sort of life he led. She didn't have much to say about herself. Her name was Sara Malone and she was 24, but that was all she volunteered.

From that point on the time flew by, and Andy was thankful that Whitey's had been closed. He wanted the evening to pass more slowly. He was happy, and he dreaded returning to his empty bed in his tiny room.

Finally she glanced at her watch, then smiled up at him. "I have to go," she said. "It's getting late."

RIDE A WHITE HORSE

"One more drink," he suggested.

"No," she said. "We've had enough. Let's go."

He helped her on with her coat and walked outside with her. He stood there on the sidewalk, awkwardly. "Sara," he said, "when can I see you again?"

She smiled, and it was a warm, easy smile. "You could come home with me. If you'd like to."

They walked quickly, with the blackness of the night around them like a blanket. And when they reached her apartment they kissed and they held each other. He took her, and lying there in her arms, with her firm breasts warm against his chest, he felt complete and whole again.

When he woke up the next morning she was already awake, and he smelled food cooking. He washed and dressed, then went into the kitchen for breakfast. It was a fine breakfast, and so very much better than toast and coffee at the Five Star Diner. He had to keep looking across the table at her to make sure that he was really awake and that she was really there. He couldn't believe what had happened, but the memory of last night was too vivid to leave room for doubt.

They didn't talk much during breakfast. He couldn't talk, afraid that he might do something to spoil it all. When he finished his second cup of coffee, he stood up regretfully.

"I have to go now," he said. "I have to be at work by 9."

"When will you be home? I'll have dinner ready."

"Right after work," he said. "About 5:15 or so. Don't you have to work?" He remembered that she hadn't mentioned it last night.

"No. I have enough money for awhile, so I don't work." She smiled. "Would you do me a favor?"

"Of course."

"I checked a package at the Public Library yesterday and forgot to pick it up on the way out. You work across the street from the library don't you?"

He nodded.

ONE NIGHT STANDS

"Here," she said. She took a ticket from her purse and handed it to him. "Will you get it for me?"

"Sure." He put the ticket in his pocket and slipped on his overcoat. He walked slowly to the door, and when he turned she was in his arms suddenly, kissing him. "I love you," he said. He walked lightly down the street, and she closed the door softly behind him.

His work went easily and quickly that day. He was anxious for five o'clock to roll around, but the memory of last night and the promise of the coming one made the time pass. At noon he picked up her parcel at the library, a small box wrapped in brown wrapping paper. He brought it home to her that night, and she put it on the top shelf in the closet.

Sara cooked him a good dinner, and he helped her with the dishes. They sat in the living-room, listening to records, until it was time for bed. Then they made love, and he knew that he could never live without her again, that he could never sleep without her beside him.

Days passed and the nights. Andy had never been so happy and contented in his life. He settled into a routine once again, but it was a groove rather than a rut. His life before had lacked only a woman like Sara to make it complete, and now nothing was missing.

From time to time he thought of asking her to marry him. But, for some reason, he was afraid to. Everything was so perfect that he was hesitant to chance changing the arrangement. He let things remain as they were.

He knew very little about her, really. She seemed reluctant to talk about her past life. She didn't say how she was able to afford the luxurious apartment they lived in, or what she did during the days while he was at the office. He didn't press her. Nothing mattered, just so long as she was there for him when he arrived home.

She had him pick up packages frequently—about twice a week or so. They were always the same type—small boxes wrapped in brown wrapping paper. Sometimes they were in a locker at the bus depot, sometimes at the library, sometimes in a safety deposit box at the bank. He wondered idly what the boxes contained, but she wouldn't

RIDE A WHITE HORSE

tell him, and he suspected it was some sort of medicine which she didn't want to mention. The question nagged at him, though. It bothered persistently. He didn't care about her earlier life, for that was beyond her now. But he wanted to know everything about her as she was now, wanted to share all of her life.

Inevitably, one evening he brought home a package and she was not home. He sat waiting for her, the package in his lap. He stared at the package, turning it over and over in his hands, as though he were trying to burn a hole in the wrapping paper with his eyes. Five, ten minutes passed, and he couldn't stand it any longer. He untied the string, removed the wrapping paper, and opened the box.

The box was filled with a white powder. He looked at it, smelled it, and tasted a flake of it. It was nothing that he could recognize. He was wondering what the devil it could be when he heard a key in the lock, and he began guiltily to re-wrap the package. Sara entered the room while he was still fussing with the string.

"Andy!" she cried. "What are you doing?"

"The package came undone," he said lamely. "I was re-wrapping it for you."

She looked at him accusingly. "Did you see what was inside?"

"Yes," he said. "What was it, Sara?"

She took the box from him. "Never mind," she said. "Just some powder."

But this time he would not be put off. He had to know. "What is it? I'll find out anyway."

She let out a sigh. I guess you had to find out. I . . ."

He waited.

"It's . . . horse, Andy."

"What!"

"Horse. Heroin."

"I know what 'horse' is," he said. "But what are you doing with it? You're not an addict, are you?" He couldn't believe what she had told him, but he knew from the expression on her face that she was telling the truth. Still, it was hard to believe, and he did not want to believe it.

"No," she said. "I'm not an addict. I'm what they call a pusher, Andy. I sell the heroin to addicts."

For a moment he could not speak. Finally he managed to say, "Why?"

She hesitated. "Money," she said. "I make lots of money. And it costs money for an apartment like this, and for good clothes and steak for dinner."

"You'll stop. I'm making enough money for us both, and you'll stop before you get caught. We'll get a smaller place somewhere and . . ."

"No," she cut in. "I won't get caught, Andy. And I want to keep on like this. I like steak, Andy. I like this place."

He stared at her. His mouth dropped open and he shook his head from side to side. "No! Sara, I won't let you!"

"I'm going to."

"I . . . I can't pick up any more packages for you."

She smiled. "Yes, you can. And you will, because you need me." She threw back her shoulders so that her breasts strained against the front of her dress. "We need each other, don't we?"

He stood up, and the package fell to the floor. He reached for her and lifted her in his arms, carrying her to the bedroom. And they came together fitfully and fiercely, as though the force of their bodies could erase everything else.

Later, when he was lying still beside her, she said, "In a way, it's better that you know. I'll need help with the business, and you can quit your job and help me. I guess it's better this way."

At that moment Andy began to distrust her. His love slowly dissolved eventually to be replaced by an ever-increasing hatred.

The following morning he quit his job. It had never been an especially exciting job, but he had liked it. He liked the office and the people he worked with. He hadn't wanted to quit.

RIDE A WHITE HORSE

But he could never give up Sara. He couldn't live without her, couldn't sleep again in an empty bed. She had become a habit, a part of his routine, and he had to have her no matter what.

The days that followed were hell for him. Sara taught him the business step-by-step, from pick-ups and deliveries to actual sales. He learned how to contact an addict and take his money from him. He watched feverish men cook the heroin on a spoon and shoot it into a vein. And he watched Sara refuse a shot to an addict without money, and watched the man beg and plead while his hands twitched and his knees shook.

He thought he would lose his mind. He argued with Sara, telling her what a rotten thing she was doing, but he couldn't sway her. He saw her for what she was—cold, mercenary, and ruthless. And in her arms at night, he couldn't believe that she was the same woman.

Bit by bit, piece by piece, he learned the business. It became a routine after awhile, but it was a routine which he hated. He settled into it, but he had trouble sleeping nights. Time after time he tried to leave her, but it was impossible.

One night he was siting in the livingroom, trying to read a magazine. She came over and sat beside him taking the magazine from his hands. She handed him a brown cigarette, loosely-packed. "Here," she said, smiling. "Smoke this."

"What! This is marijuana, isn't it?"

"That's right. Smoke it."

"Are you crazy?"

She smiled slowly and ran her hand up and down his thigh. "Don't be silly. I've been smoking pot for a long time now, and it doesn't hurt you. It makes you feel real fine. Try it?"

He drew away from her, his eyes searching hers. "I don't want to become an addict, Sara. I've seen the poor fish suffer, and I don't want it."

She laughed. "It's not habit-forming. I've been smoking since I was 17, and I just have a joint whenever I want one. You want to stay clear of horse, but this won't hurt you."

ONE NIGHT STANDS

He drew a deep breath. "No," he said, firmly. "I don't want it."

Her hand worked on his thigh, and with her other hand she toyed with the buttons on her blouse. "You want me, though," she said, huskily. "Don't you, Andy?"

She put the cigarette between his lips and lit it, and made him smoke it quickly, drawing the pungent, acrid smoke deep into his lungs. At first he was dizzy; then his stomach churned and he was sick. But she only made him smoke another, and this time the smoke took hold of him and held him, and the room grew large and small and large again, and he made love to her with a thousand voices shrieking warning inside his brain.

And so marijuana, too, became a part of Andy's routine. He smoked as an alcoholic drank, losing his worries in the smoke. It was more a habit with him than it was with Sara. He grew to depend upon it, mentally if not physically.

And he learned things, too. He learned to smoke the joint down to a "roach," or butt, in order to get the maximum charge from it. He learned to hold as much smoke as he could in his lungs for as long as possible, in order to intensify the effect. He learned to smoke two or three joints in a row.

At the same time, he learned his business from start to finish. He bargained with contacts and squeezed the last cent from customers, burying his conscience completely. He gained an understanding of the operations of the narcotics racket, from the Big Man to the small-time pusher. Everything he did became part of him, and part of his routine.

He sat alone in the apartment one day, just after selling a cap of heroine to an addict. He opened a glassine envelope and idly poked the powder with the point of a pencil.

Horse, he thought. White Horse, the same as the bar where they had met. Valuable stuff. People killed for it, went through hell for it.

He sat looking at it for a long time, and then he folded a slip of paper and poured some of the powder on it. He raised the paper to his

RIDE A WHITE HORSE

nose, closed his eyes, and sniffed deeply. He drew the flakes through his nostrils and into his lungs, and the heroin hit home.

It was a new sensation, a much bigger charge than marijuana had given him. He liked it. He threw away the slip of paper, put the heroin away, and leaned back to relax. Everything was pink and fuzzy, soft and smooth and cool.

He started sniffing heroin daily, and soon he noticed that he was physically aware of it when it was time for a fix. He began increasing the dosage, as his body began to demand more of the drug. And he didn't tell Sara anything about it.

His hate for her had grown, but it too became habitual. He learned to live with it. However, when they had a disagreement over the business, he realized that she was standing in the way.

Andy wanted to expand operations. He saw that, with a little effort and a little muscle, he and Sara could move up a notch and have a crowd of pushers under them. He explained it to her, step by step. It couldn't miss.

"No," she said, flatly. "We're doing fine right where we are. We make good money and nobody will want us out of the way."

"We could make more money," he said. "Lots more. The cops wouldn't be able to touch us."

"It's a risk."

He shrugged. "Everything's a risk. Walking across the street is a risk, but you can't stay on your own block forever. It's a chance we've got to take."

She refused, and once again she used her body as a bargaining point. At last he gave in, as always, but the hate was beginning to boil in him.

A few days later an addict came whining for a shot. Andy saw the way he trembled and twitched, but the spectacle didn't bother him any longer. He had seen it time and time again, until it was just a part of the day's work.

"Sorry, junkie," he said. "Come back when you raise the dough."

ONE NIGHT STANDS

The man begged, and Andy started to push him out the door when a thought came to him. He opened the door and let the man in.

"C'mere," he said. "You got a spike?"

The addict nodded dumbly and pulled a hypodermic needle from his pocket. Andy took it from him and inspected it, turning it over and over in his hand. "Okay," he said at length. "A shot for your spike."

The man sighed with relief, then demanded, "How am I gonna take the shot without a spike?"

"Take it first; then get out."

Andy followed the addict into the bathroom and watched him heat the powder on a spoon. Then he filled the syringe and shot it into the vein in his arm. It hit immediately, and he relaxed.

"Thanks," he said. He handed the syringe to Andy. "Thanks."

"Get out." The addict left, and Andy closed the door after him.

He washed the syringe in hot water, then put some heroin on a spoon. He deftly filled the syringe and gave himself a shot in the fleshy part of his arm.

It was far more satisfying than sniffing the powder. It was stronger and faster. He felt good.

As the heroin became more and more a part of his life, he switched to the mainline, shooting it directly into the vein. It was necessary to him now, and he itched to build up his trade until he controlled narcotics in the town. He knew he could handle it. Already, he had virtually replaced Sara. She was the messenger now, while he handled the important end. But she still called the shots, for she still held the trump card. And no matter how he argued, she would simply rub herself up against him and kiss him, and the argument would be finished. So he could do nothing but wait.

And, at last, he was one day ready.

He took a long, sharp knife from the kitchen drawer and walked slowly to the bedroom, where she lay reading. She looked up from the magazine and smiled at him, stretching languorously.

"Hi," she said. "What's up?"

RIDE A WHITE HORSE

He returned the smile, keeping the knife behind his back. "I have news for you," he said. "We're expanding, like I suggested. No more small-time stuff, Sara."

She sighed. "Not again, Andy. I told you before..."

"This time *I'm* telling *you*."

"Oh," she said, amused. "Do you think you can get along without me?"

"I know I can."

"Really?" She threw back the bedcovers and smiled up at him. "You need me, Andy."

He forced himself to look at her. He ran his eyes over the firm breasts, the soft curves of her hips. He looked at her carefully, waiting for the familiar stir within him. It didn't come.

"I don't need you," he said, slowly, "Look."

He held out his right hand, the hand that held the knife. He unbuttoned the sleeve and rolled it down slowly, showing her the marks of the needle. "See? I'm a junkie, Sara. I only care about one thing, baby, and it isn't you. You don't show me a thing."

But her eyes were not on the marks on his arm. They were on the knife in his hand, and they were wide with fear.

"I don't need you at all," he went on. "I don't need liquor, I don't need sex, I don't need you. You're just dead wood, Sara."

She rose from the bed and moved toward him. "Andy," she cooed. "Andy, honey." Her whole body seemed to reach out for him, hungrily.

He shook his head. "Sorry," he said. "It just won't work anymore. I don't care about it. Just the horse is all that matters."

She looked into his eyes, and they were flat and uncaring. "Wait," she said. "We'll play it your way, Andy. We'll expand, like you said. Anything you say."

"You don't understand. I don't *need* you."

"Please!" she moaned. "Please!"

"Sorry. It's time for my shot." And he lowered the knife.

171

ONE NIGHT STANDS

He moved toward her and she tried to back away, but he kept coming, the knife pointed at her. "No!" she shrieked. And she started to say something else, but before she could get the words out the knife was in her heart.

A SHROUD FOR THE DAMNED

Sigmund opened the door slowly and tiptoed inside. The door squeaked shut behind him as he headed for his room. The night was still and dark and Sigmund was very tired. He wanted to sleep.

"Sigmund!" He started at the voice.

She was sitting in the red armchair. At least it had been red once, many years and several owners ago. With the passage of time the color had faded almost entirely away, and in the dim lamplight the chair was an unimaginative gray. And she looked gray in the lamplight, with her hands so busy and her eyes so still. She looked as gray and as shop-worn as the old armchair.

"Hi, Ma," he said. "I thought you'd be sleeping." He smiled automatically and started once again for his room.

"Sigmund!" The voice caught him, halted him in his tracks, and turned him toward her once more.

"Come here, Sigmund."

He tiptoed at first, until he realized that she was awake and that she had seen him, and he had no reason to walk softly. He crossed to the side of the old armchair and stood there awkwardly, looking down at her, waiting for her to speak.

"Sit down," she said. "In the other chair. Sit down so your mother can talk to you. You're so tall I can't talk to you when you stand up. You grew fast this last year, Sigmund."

He started to protest, started to tell her how tired he was, then gave it up and took the seat across from her. He sat, watching her, and if her hands had not been moving all the while he would have thought that she were sleeping. But her hands moved, quick and sure, and they were as much alive as her eyes were dead.

"Sigmund," she said at last, "you were out late."

He looked away. "It's not so late."

ONE NIGHT STANDS

"Late," she said, firmly. "You should come home early and be with your mother. Then maybe you could wake up mornings. It's not good you should sleep so late in the mornings." He didn't say anything. He started to tap his foot on the floor, slowly and rhythmically, but after a few experimental taps the foot stopped by itself.

"You know what I'm doing?"

"Knitting," he said.

"Smart boy. And do you know what I'm knitting?"

He shook his head, desiring only to end the conversation and crawl into his warm bed. But she had no one else to talk to, and she seemed so horribly alone, always looking desperately and methodically for something which was no longer present.

"You don't know," she said, accusingly. "In the old country you would know, but here..." She shrugged briefly and left the sentence dangling, unfinished.

Here we go, he thought. The old country bit again. You'd think she was still living there.

"It's a shroud," she said. "You know what's a shroud for?"

"Yeah. It's for when someone dies."

She nodded. "To wrap them. In the old country, when a person dies he was wrapped in a shroud before they buried him. It was to keep out the spirits."

He looked at her hands and watched the long knitting needles flash back and forth. All right, he thought. But so what?

"Not here, " she continued. "Not in this country, where they bury a man in a suit. Does it make sense? A suit? This will keep out spirits?"

He didn't answer, nor did she wait for an answer. "Your father once said that a person who made shrouds and grew food would never grow hungry. You understand?"

He didn't, but nodded anyway.

"Because," she said triumphantly, "if people lived, he sold food, and if they died, he sold shrouds. You understand?"

"Sure. I understand."

A SHROUD FOR THE DAMNED

"But not in this country. Here they bury men in suits. Here a boy sixteen years old thinks just because he's tall he can stay out all night. It isn't right that children should come home so late."

He sighed. "Look, Ma. Listen a minute, will you? People don't buy shrouds here and you can't grow food in a crack in the sidewalk. You know what I mean?" His voice rose involuntarily and he lowered it.

"Ma, we have to eat. You can't sell your shrouds, and we have to eat. I brought money for you." He pulled some bills from his pocket and held them out to her.

She closed her eyes and silently refused the money. "Where did you get it, Sigmund?"

He looked away. "I got it. What's the difference where?"

She darted a look at him, and for an instant there was life again in her eyes. Then they were dull once more, dull and flat and tired. "You stole it," she said. "You are a thief."

He tightened his hands into fists and remained silent.

"My son is a thief. My son Sigmund stole money. A thief." And then she too was silent. . .

The silence came over him like a dark woolly blanket, more accusing than anything she could say. He had to break it. "Ma," he said at last, "don't you understand? Don't you?"

"I understand only that you are a thief."

"We need the money to live. You won't let me quit school and get a job . . ."

"A boy should go to school," she said.

"And you won't let me take a job on Saturdays . . ."

"No son of mine will work on the Sabbath."

"And you won't take the relief money . . ."

"Charity," she broke in. "Charity I don't want."

"And you don't have a job. So I have to steal, Ma. What else can I do?"

ONE NIGHT STANDS

She didn't seem to hear his question. "I would work," she said slowly. "I would have a job. No one will hire me, not in this country."

Her eyes closed then, and only her hands moved. It was the same argument, the same words that Sigmund had heard a hundred times in the past. Either he would be a thief or she would go hungry, it was that simple.

He stood up and walked quietly to the kitchen. He took the lid from the cookie jar and noted that only a handful of change remained. She could spend it well enough, even if she never took it directly from him or acknowledged the source of the money. He grinned sadly and placed the bills in the jar.

He slept well that night. There were dreams, unpleasant ones, but he was tired enough to sleep anyway and he didn't hear the alarm clock in the morning. And once again he was almost an hour late for school.

School ended, finally. The classes were dull and the teachers were something of a nuisance, but Sigmund clenched his hands into fists and lived through it, just as he lived through the flight from Poland long ago. He would clench his hands into tight little fists, and sometimes lower his eyelids, and everything passed in time.

Lucci was waiting for him after school. Lucci was the same age but not as tall as Sigmund. But Lucci's mother was dead and Lucci's father drank red wine all day, so Lucci did not go to school.

"Tonight," Lucci said. "We'll go out tonight, okay?"

Sigmund hesitated. "It's cold out. It'll be cold as ice tonight."

"So what? You can use the gold, can't you?"

Sigmund nodded.

"So we'll go out then. Want to shoot some pool?"

"I can't," said Sigmund. "No money."

Lucci shrugged. "What the hell, we're buddies, aren't we? I'll treat."

A SHROUD FOR THE DAMNED

They were buddies, and they went to the small pool-room on Christie Street where the cigar smoke was thick and warm in the air. They played two games of 8-ball and one game of straight and one game of Chicago, and they each smoked two of Lucci's cigarettes, and Lucci paid for all the games. Then it was time to go. They shook hands warmly because they were buddies and Sigmund walked home for his dinner. It was so cold on the street that he could see his breath in front of his eyes, hovering in the air like the cigar smoke in the pool-room. He shuddered.

When he opened the door he could smell food cooking on the stove, but otherwise he would not have known that his mother had moved at all since the previous night. She was sitting again in the red armchair, her fingers flying as they skillfully manipulated the slender needles. She looked up as he came in.

"It is cold out," she said. "You are almost blue from the cold, Sigmund."

He rubbed his hands together. "It's not that bad." He took off his jacket and hung it on a peg on the wall. When he turned around she was holding her knitting up proudly.

"Look," she said. "It's almost finished. Weeks I have worked on it, and it's almost finished."

He forced himself to smile. "That's good. That's real good, Ma."

"Tonight it will be done. She stood up slowly and beckoned to him. "Come, let us eat."

The food was good. There was tender boiled cabbage and lamb stew and milk, and Sigmund enjoyed the meal. He ate quickly despite her frequent injunctions to chew his food more thoroughly, and he stood up from the table as soon as he was finished.

"That was a good meal, Ma."

She frowned at him. "Where are you going? You're not going out, Sigmund?"

"Yeah. There's a guy I have to meet."

"No," she said. "Not one of your hoodlum friends, not in this weather. It's too cold for your hoodlum friends."

ONE NIGHT STANDS

"I've got to go out," he said, uncomfortably. "It's not that cold."

"All night you'll be out. All night you'll be freezing in the cold with your hoodlums. Don't go, please."

He leaned over and pecked at her forehead. "Good-bye, Ma. I'll try to be home early." He grabbed his jacket from the peg and hurried out the door, managing to escape her final words.

The night was cold and the wind blew through the thin jacket. But Lucci was waiting at the corner, a smile playing on his thin lips, a light dancing in his eyes. "It's too early," Lucci said. "Let's have a game of pool."

They played two games of 8-ball and a game of Chicago at the Place on Chrisite Street. Sigmund lost all three games, as he always lost when they played, and Lucci paid for all three, as he always paid. Then Lucci said it was time enough, and they set the cue sticks on the table-top and hurried into the night.

They walked west, through the cold clutter of the streets toward the Bowery. "This is the ticket," Lucci explained. "You just give a drunk a tap on the head and he's out for the night. Just a little tap and we take his gold. But don't tap too hard, 'cause they get soft in the head from drinking, and you'll squash their heads like a melon."

Sigmund saw a drunk, weaving back and forth along the sidewalk. "Him?"

"No, too seedy. You got to pick a guy with money."

They walked on, passing up some as too run-down and other's as too sober, until Lucci saw a victim. They surrounded the man and Lucci chopped him across the temple and the man went to the ground without protest. It was very easy.

But the drunk's pockets yielded only seven dollars and change, so they kept on looking. The wind grew colder and colder, and few men were on the streets, but they didn't give up.

They saw the man then, out of place on the Bowery. They walked up behind him and Sigmund hit him hard on the head, but the man

178

A SHROUD FOR THE DAMNED

did not lose consciousness as the other had. Instead he stared up from the sidewalk and opened his mouth to scream.

Lucci kicked him, a short, hard kick in the side of the head. The man's head rolled slightly on the pavement, his eyes closed, and he died.

"Christ!" said Lucci. He grabbed for the man's wallet and they ran in panic down the street. At the corner they divided the money and split up.

Sigmund's share for the night was sixty dollars. It was more money than he had ever had before, more money than he had seen in a long time. But the man was dead and cold on the cold sidewalk, and the icy wind could not stop the sweat from forming steadily on Sigmund's brow.

The man was dead. The thought was colder than the wind, and the wind was very cold.

He opened the door and tiptoed inside, softly. The door squeaked shut behind him and she looked up across the room from the faded red armchair. Although her eyes were flat and lifeless, they seemed to look right through him.

"Sigmund," she said.

He rubbed his hands together to warm them. He was cold very cold. He took off his jacket and hung it on the peg.

"You're cold," she said. "On a night like this you had to go out. Stealing, on a night like this."

She looked into his eyes then, and he returned the look. For a moment her eyes were alive again, burning into him. But the life vanished as suddenly as it had appeared.

"I want to go to sleep," he said. "Ma, I . . . I want to go right to sleep."

She took a deep breath and released it slowly, almost as though she were reluctant to let go of it. Then she stood up, slowly, lifting the black garment and holding it in front of her. "Sigmund, tonight you'll be cold. It's a cold night, this one."

ONE NIGHT STANDS

He was shivering. "I know. That's why I want to go to bed now."

"Do me a favor. Wear this." She reached out her hands, offering the shroud to him. "Do it for your mother."

"What for?"

"It's warm. Believe me, it's a warm thing."

"But it's a shroud, Ma."

"So? In this country, it's just something else to wrap in. They don't have shrouds, not in this country."

He started to back away. "I don't need it. Honest."

"Take it," she said. "Tight stitching it's got, so it should be warm. Please."

He shrugged and took the shroud from her, then hurried to his room. He undressed rapidly, wrapped himself in the shroud, and got into bed. It was warm, anyhow, and it was a very cold night.

She stayed for a long time in the red armchair. She sat very still, and now even her hands were motionless. Time passed slowly.

She stood up at last and walked to his room. The door was slightly ajar. She pushed it open and entered.

"Sigmund," she whispered. "Are you asleep?"

There was no answer. He lay very still, not tossing as much as he had done on recent nights. The shroud was wrapped neatly around him, almost covering his face.

"Sigmund," she repeated, and again there was no response.

She looked then, at the knitting needle that she held in her right hand. She looked at it for several minutes, and she knew what had to be done. She would do it swiftly, just as her husband had done to the German many years ago.

Carefully she lifted the blanket back, exposing the shrouded form. Then, in one motion, she jabbed the long slender needle through the shroud and into the body at the base of the spine. The boy twitched once, as the German had done, and then lay still.

She pulled out the knitting needle and washed it in the sink. Then she returned to the faded red armchair and sat in it, thinking. He

A SHROUD FOR THE DAMNED

would be warm now. The shroud would keep him warm. And he would be good, for the shroud would keep the evil spirits from him.

After some time she picked up the needles and her ball of yarn. She began to knit again, and at first her fingers moved very slowly. Gradually they picked up speed, and her hands moved faster and faster.

SWEET LITTLE RACKET

The newspaper seemed to open by itself to the classified ads. You get that way after awhile. You get so used to fumbling through the paper every morning, hunting for a job, then folding the paper up and throwing it against the wall. It's a regular routine—not the greatest bit in the world—but one that sort of grows on you when you go long enough without working.

I was sick of it. I ran my eyes down the column but there was nothing, nothing worth wasting my time on. I folded the paper methodically and flung it against the wall. It didn't help; I still felt lousy.

If I were just a punk I wouldn't mind it, but I wasn't used to wasting my time sitting around a crummy room. I was never rich, but I used to have a red-hot little liquor store that made nice money.

I cut prices and did a volume business until they brought in Fair Trade and knocked the business to hell. Then the heavy taxes on small businesses made things just that much worse. Bit by bit the business fell apart.

Five months. Five months without working, five months doing nothing, and all because the big boys had things rigged against the little man. I could have gone out and grabbed a two-bit job, but there's no sense working for somebody else. You never get any place that way.

I stood up, ready to go down the street for a beer before the landlady came around and yelled for the rent, when the idea hit me. I just couldn't go on like this an more. And I hit on a way to set up a handy little business all my own, a business the big boys couldn't pull out from under me.

The big boys had the world nicely wrapped around their pinkies. But when everything stacks up so perfectly for you, that's the time

SWEET LITTLE RACKET

you have to be careful. You scare easy. You hedge your bets and quit taking the chances that brought you to the top.

All I needed was a couple of big boys who were afraid. If I could scare five of them to the tune of fifty bucks a week, I would be set up with a little business pulling down two and a half yards per. And that was handy money to a loner like me. No wife and kids to feed—no folks to support—it could be big dough. And the big boys can afford fifty a week with no headaches.

The first big boy I wanted to get was Gargan. James Gargan of Gargan motors, the fat slob who repossessed my buggy when I fell a few months back in the payments. He could afford the fifty, that was certain enough. And I'd like to be sitting on his payroll.

I drafted a letter to Gargan and read it over. It looked good—simple and to the point. He was to mail fifty dollars a week to me, or one of his kids might get hit by a car. Nice and simple. I could picture his face while he read the letter. First he'd think it was a bluff. Then he'd start wondering. And finally he'd decide it didn't matter whether it was a bluff or not. Hell, he couldn't chance anything happening to one of his kids, could he?

And the next thing he knew, he'd be slipping a brand-new fifty in an envelope and addressing it to me.

You know I almost mailed that letter. I was halfway down the street to the mailbox before I realized what a stupid play that would be. I remembered reading somewhere that there were two kinds of blackmail, the only difference being whether the threat came by letter or in person. By letter was a felony; in person was only a misdemeanor. Sending that letter would have been one of the dumbest things ever.

Instead, I walked into Mr. Gargan's office that afternoon. I gave him the pitch, laying it right on the line. Then I leaned back in my chair and stared at him.

For several minutes be didn't say anything, but I could hear his mind working it out. Then he blew a cloud of cigar smoke at the ceiling and said, "I suppose you know this is blackmail."

ONE NIGHT STANDS

I just smiled in his face.

"I could have you arrested," he went on. "I could call a policeman and have you arrested immediately."

"How would you prove it?"

"They'd take my word for it."

I shrugged. "You're a smart man, Mr. Gargan. You don't figure I'm working this all by myself, do you? If you lock me up, your kid'll get it just the same."

He chewed on the cigar and I wondered whether he'd have the guts to call my bluff. But he didn't.

"Fifty dollars?"

I nodded.

"I'm to send it to you?"

I shook my head. "No," I said. "I'll pick it up every Monday afternoon, and you can start the ball rolling this afternoon. Just put me on your payroll for fifty bucks."

"You bastard," he said. He considered for another moment and stood up, reaching in his pocket for his wallet. He slipped me two twenties and a ten and swore at me again.

"It's just a business," I told him. "Don't take it so hard, Mr. Gargan." Before he could answer I turned around and walked out.

One time at the liquor store I jabbed a hypodermic needle through the corks in half a dozen bottles of imported Scotch, drained them dry, and filled them again with a cheap blend. That had been easy money, but the fifty bucks I had in my pocket right now was the easiest money ever. And it was steady: Gargan would kick in with fifty every Monday, without even whimpering from here on in.

I paid off the landlady and bought a couple shirts. I took a girl to my room for the evening. That damn near shot the fifty, but I wasn't figuring on living the rest of my life on fifty dollars per. $250 would be a lot more like it.

I picked another customer Tuesday, a guy named Theodore Sims. He ran a big insurance agency on Wilkin Street, and I came on telling him I wanted to sell him some insurance. He tried to hustle me out

SWEET LITTLE RACKET

the door, but by the time I finished my spiel he was sitting down again and doing some heavy thinking. I walked out of there ten minutes later with another fifty in my pocket and another client on my list.

Choosing my customers was the most important part. If I picked a guy who couldn't drop fifty a week without noticing it, I'd get in trouble eventually. If I tabbed a muscle boy with more guts than brains, my bluff wouldn't stand a chance.

But I was careful.

I added my name to another payroll on Wednesday and another on Thursday. Both times I spruced up my pitch a little, starting off with the insurance salesman bit and moving right into the regular routine. I got smoother and smoother, until by Friday I had myself believing that they were in for trouble if they didn't come across.

Of course, no matter what they did they were safer than a virgin in a roomful of eunuchs. I wasn't going to take a swipe at anybody's kid, and I didn't even have a car to run a kid down with if I felt like, it. But the big boys don't have to take chances, and that's why I cleared two hundred bucks the first week.

Friday was a day of rest. I had plenty of time to find a fifth sucker, and besides it was a good day to go to the beach. I took a quick dip in the water and spread out a blanket on the sand, letting the sun burn down on me and thinking what a nice little business I had. The nicest thing was the absence of competition. There was no heavy operator to push me out of the catbird's seat.

On Monday, Gargan started to make noises until I reminded him that I could always raise the ante if he didn't behave himself. The others were respectfully quiet. Another week, another two hundred for me—and with no taxes to pay. Who could ask for a better set-up?

Two hundred was enough, when you came right down to it. I'm not a guy with expensive tastes. Sure, I like a drink when I'm dry and a woman now and then, and I like expensive Scotch and high-priced women, but two hundred a week will buy plenty of liquor and sex. I'm not a pig.

185

ONE NIGHT STANDS

It went on that way for about two months. It was a regular routine: Gargan on Monday, Sims on Tuesday, Lon Butler on Wednesday, and David Clark on Thursday. I had regular working hours, and my wages came to something like fifty bucks an hour.

It even became a routine for my customers. After awhile we didn't even bother to talk to each other. I walked into the office, picked up my money, and walked out. That was all there was to it.

My landlady was thrilled. She got her rent right on the button without asking twice, and she never had it so good. She must have wondered where the hell I was getting the dough, but that was none of her business and she had enough sense to keep her nose out. She was strictly business. As long as I paid on time, she kept her eyes closed and her mouth shut.

That was the main reason I kept on living in my little dump. But I found other things to spend the money on. I picked up on an Italian silk suit and some decent shoes, bought a radio for the room, and even got some pictures for the walls. I gave one of my broads a silk night-gown and she was extra-good to me from that point on.

I even bought a car. With a steady income, it was no headache keeping up payments. I latched onto a little foreign job with wire wheels and plenty of speed. It was nice, sitting behind the wheel of the car and opening her up. It was particularly nice when I stopped to think how the car was being paid for.

Nice, huh?

But after a while the idea of another half a yard a week began looking better and better. I could get along without it all right, but fifty bucks more wouldn't hurt. I took my time, trying to pick the perfect mark. I was set up so perfectly that there was no point in risking everything unless I had a sure thing. I took my time and waited.

And I found my mark.

He was a doctor, a rich man's doctor by the name of Alfred Sanders. He had a good-looking wife and a little boy named Jerry. He loved his wife he loved his kid. It looked pretty perfect.

SWEET LITTLE RACKET

I called Doctor Sanders during the week and made an appointment for Friday afternoon. He had a spot open, and that struck me as funny. My only open afternoon, and he could fit me in!

His layout on Middlesex Road was something to see—brick front, a lawn like a putting green, and rugs on the floor that you could get lost in. His nurse showed me into the office and I took a seat.

"I'm selling insurance," I began.

He smiled. "I wish you had told me over the phone," he said. "I'm sorry, Mr. Boyle, but I have all the insurance I need. As a matter of fact, I'm probably overinsured as it stands. You see—"

"Not this kind of insurance." And then I let him have it from beginning to end.

"I see," he said when I finished. He stood up and began pacing the floor slowly, swinging his arms as he walked. "Could you give me a quick run-down on your proposition again? I missed some of the details."

I gave it to him again. Hell, I had all the time in the world.

When I got through he asked me a few questions, and I fed him the answers. I tried to sound as tough as I could. It wasn't hard; I had the whole business down pat by now.

"That should do it," be said suddenly, grinning. "I want you to hear something, Mr. Boyle. I believe you'll find it interesting."

He walked over to a cabinet on the wall that be had passed while pacing the floor. He opened the cabinet, and I saw a tape recorder with the spools revolving slowly. My eyes almost fell out of my head.

His grin widened. "Do you understand, Mr. Boyle? Or should I play it back for you?"

I started sweating. "Okay," I said. "So what does it get you? You can't call copper or my associate will play rough with Jerry. So where are you, Doc?"

"That's true," he said. "But you don't get your pound of flesh, do you? Not while I have this on tape. Fifty dollars a week would

ONE NIGHT STANDS

hardly send me to the workhouse, Mr. Boyle. But I don't like blackmailers and I don't plan on paying blackmail. Get out!"

I got out. I got out in a hurry, not wasting time to get in a last word. I was lucky to get out, for that matter. He had me by the throat, and the baloney about an "associate" was the only thing that saved me from a blackmail rap.

What the hell, $200 was plenty. I still had enough to pay for the car and the liquor and the women and the rent, and I didn't need the extra fifty, not really. It would have been nice but I learned a lesson from it. I wouldn't get greedy any more.

I stayed in my room, all night, thinking how lucky I was and how I nearly shot everything to hell. At one point I started to shake. Here I was with a perfect racket, and a stupid try for fifty bucks I didn't even need nearly bollixed up the works.

That was yesterday. Today was Saturday, and it was another good day for the beach. I thought of calling up a woman but I figured it would be a good day to be alone. A few minutes after noon I hopped into the sportscar and headed for the beach. I found a little spot all to myself and took it easy, getting through the whole day without bumping into anyone I knew or starting a conversation with anybody.

I was feeling good by the time I got back from the beach. The afternoon all by myself did it. That and the sun and the water got my mind off Doctor Sanders and the way I had balled things up. It was dark out by the time I parked the car out in front and walked up the stairs to my room.

I chalked up yesterday's goof to profit and loss. Hell, the best small business in the world can't come out ahead every time.

I stretched out on the bed and turned on the radio. It came on in the middle of a newscast, and I reached for the dial to try and get some music. News always bores the hell out of me, and after lying in the sun all day I just wanted to listen to some music and relax. I got my hand on the dial and was ready to turn it, but the news item

SWEET LITTLE RACKET

got through to me just in time. My fingers let go of the dial as if it was red hot.

It was a fairly ordinary news item, about some kid who got gunned down by a car that afternoon while I was at the beach.

It seems the kid's name was Jerry Sanders.

It seems the car was a little foreign job with wire wheels.

The radio's going now. I can't concentrate on the music too well, because all I can think of is how no matter how good a business you set up, something's going to pull it out from under you.

The cops should be here any minute.

THE WAY TO POWER

He opened the door in his bathrobe and motioned me inside. "Have a seat, Joe," he said, "Relax a little."

I took a seat, and it was easy to relax in the soft, plush cushions. I looked around the room and the familiar feeling of awe hit me. I had been to his house maybe a thousand times, but I never missed feeling the lushness of the place.

"Drink?"

I nodded, and went on filling my eyes while he went for drinks. I took it all in, from the Mexican jade on the mantel to the ivory-and-ebony chess table. He had done well. Damned well.

He brought the drinks, and I forced myself to sip mine, rather than throw it straight down. It was Scotch, and straight from Scotland. Nothing but the best for him, ever.

I looked up at him from my drink. He had taken a seat in an equally plush chair across from me, and was waiting expectantly. I played the game.

"Thanks, Chief. What's up?"

"Lucci. He doesn't understand."

I knew what he was talking about, but I also knew how he liked to play it. "What do you mean Chief?"

"Phil Lucci," he said. "Remember I mentioned him?"

"I remember."

His eyes narrowed, until I could hardly see the red veins that mapped them. "He's making book, still. Three weeks ago he was told to pay off or lay off, one or the other. He wouldn't join the mob, and he wouldn't quit taking bets. You know what that means, Joe."

I knew, of course. The Chief was about as subtle as a Coney Island prostitute. But the Chief ran every racket in Central City, and

THE WAY TO POWER

he had the town in his pocket. So when the chief wanted to tell me something, I let him tell me.

"He's gotta lose," he said. "He has to lose all the way, the big loss." He paused for effect, but I was so used to the gesture that it was lost on me. "Joe, Lucci's gotta die."

I could have dropped it there, but he would have missed all his fun. He was all keyed up for his big speech, and I couldn't afford to let him down. His eyes were waiting, expectant. So I let him have his kicks.

"Why, Chief? All he's costing us is maybe ten bucks a day. Why do we rub him out?"

He stood up then. He stood up and threw what was left of the imported Scotch straight into his stomach, and his eyes were shining. "Power," he said, and the word seemed to come from the inside of a bass drum. "Power," he repeated.

"Joe," he went on, "the money doesn't matter. Oh, it's nice to have, but if you worry about it you're through. The money is just the chips in the pot, just a way to keep score. The thing is, you have to be on top. You have to have power.

"There was this German guy named Nietzsche who figured it all out, and for a Square-head he made a lot of sense. He said the important thing, the thing that makes a man superior, is his Will to Power. A man who wants to be on top, just for the hell of it, he's the guy to be."

He paused for a breath, and I finished my drink. "A smart guy," he said. "I read every one of his books."

He had told me this at least twenty times. "Every one?" I marveled.

"Every one. Every God-damned one." He sat down heavily in his seat and let out a deep sigh. Evidently the performance had exhausted him.

"Joe," he said, "I can't let anyone get in the way. I gotta stay on top. I gotta keep every bit of my power, and that's why Lucci has to die. Does that make sense?"

ONE NIGHT STANDS

"Damn good sense."

"You said it, boy. You said it." He seemed almost relieved, as if he had expected me to argue with him.

"Look, Chief," I said, when he didn't say anything, "what do you expect from me? I mean, you don't want me to gun him, do you? I will if you want, but I'm not a torpedo."

"No, I don't want you for that. I got a million guns. But I don't want him gunned at all. Dammit, Joe, we can't risk another shooting. We've had five already this year."

"I don't get it," I said, because I didn't. "Chief, you have the whole force in your pocket. If you give the word, every cop in town buries his head in the sand and stuffs cotton in his ears. What's the worry over a shooting?"

He shook his head. "Sure I've got the cops. But the citizens don't know this. The citizens don't understand how the ball bounces. When there are enough unsolved homicides, they get upset. They switch mayors. They switch cops. They switch everything. And then where the hell am I?"

I nodded slowly. He was no moron. He had used his head to get where he was.

"I want to nail him sort of indirect," he said. "But I'm not sure how. That's why I called you. Figure a way."

I closed my eyes and began stroking my chin with my left hand. This was one of the big reasons he tolerated me—he was convinced I was a thinker. He would have me come to his house and think until I told him what he had already said, and he knew then that I must be a genius.

I made him feel powerful, and he liked that. That's the only reason he tolerated anyone. Ruthie made him feel powerful too. She would crawl on her belly to him, begging him to take her. The last girl he had didn't crawl to him one night, and he got irritated and broke her back. So Ruthie crawls, and I can't really blame her.

THE WAY TO POWER

But she didn't always crawl for him. There was a time when she would have crawled to me, and not because she was afraid of getting a broken back. But that was a long time ago.

So I stroked my chin like a baboon and thought. It was more difficult than usual, since I didn't have the slightest idea what he wanted me to suggest. He seemed to want me to come up with an idea all on my own.

And I did. It was strange, for it was about the first idea I had ever had all by myself, at least since I started working for the Chief. But I had an idea, and the more I thought about it the better it sounded. I opened my eyes and looked up at him. He was waiting.

"I got it," I said. "We'll frame him."

The Chief got a happy look in his eyes. He liked new gimmicks, and this sounded like a fairly new way to take a boy for a ride. "Go on," he said. "Go on Joe."

"We'll frame him for murder," I said. "We'll knock off someone, some Skid Row bum, and we'll tie it to him. The cops will pick him up right away, because you'll tell them to. And we'll have thirty guys swear they saw Lucci kill the guy. And you'll tell the judge to hang him, and he will."

He hesitated, and I gave him the clincher. "You've got the power," I said, reverently. "You can pull something like this off perfectly."

That did it, of course. *Power* was the magic word to the Chief. "Yes," he said, sliding the word over his tongue. "I *could* do it. And it would be perfect, wouldn't it?"

I nodded.

"Yes," he repeated. "Perfect." He smiled a big, oily smile. "When do you want to pull it off?"

"Tonight!" I practically shouted the word. His enthusiasm was suddenly contagious, and this time it was *my* idea. I was all caught up in the beauty of it.

"Tonight?" He smiled. "Okay, Joe. Who do you think ought to gun the tramp?"

ONE NIGHT STANDS

I thought a moment, and although I didn't want to come up with the answer I couldn't help myself. "I'll do it," I said, calmly. "The less people on to this caper, the better it is. I'll fix it."

He smiled wider this time. "Now you're talking," he said. "You're starting to understand what power means, Joe. I'll get you a gun."

He vanished and came back in a minute. "Here you go," he said, handing me a light-weight .38 automatic. "It's clean, Joe. No registration, no nothing. Just wipe it off and drop it, and it might as well be Lucci's as anyone else's."

I took it from him and fitted it to my grip. It felt good. I pocketed it and stood up. "Okay," I said. "I'll be right back, by 9:30 at the latest. Wait up for me and we can talk over the next part, huh?"

"That's the ticket," he said. "I'll be waiting right here. Of course," he added, "I may have to go upstairs and spend a few minutes with Ruthie." He winked. "She'd go nuts otherwise."

I smiled nervously, shook hands with him, and walked down the long driveway to my car. It was a fine car, a new Pontiac, and while it didn't measure up to his Caddy, it got me wherever I was going. It was one of the benefits of being the Chief's lieutenant.

That, and a good apartment, and money in the bank. The only loss involved had been Ruthie, and I stopped caring about her after the first month or so. She was just a woman, and the world is full of them. There were other things that were much more important. Power, perhaps. The Chief and Nietzsche had something there.

I drove onto Clinton Street and down toward the waterfront. It was only a little way to Skid Row, the street of broken dreams and broken men. It was the place where nobody really cared about anything, and where everyone waited hopefully for death. Killing a wino would hardly seem like murder. The poor sonofabitch would neither know nor care what happened to him.

I drove slowly once I hit Halsey Street. I didn't want to park the car and chase around on foot. I wanted one good shot from the front

THE WAY TO POWER

window. Then I would drive like hell for two blocks, then slow down and head back to the Chief's home. It would be simple enough.

I circled up and down the Row a good four or five times, and I never managed to get off a shot. There were either too many lights or not enough light to see by, either a crowd of bums or no bums at all.

I was almost ready to give up for the night, when I got another idea, an original idea. It was my second original idea of the evening, and I just couldn't pass it up. It was a good idea too. So, I drove part way back on Clinton and made a phone call at a drugstore.

I returned to the Chief's place at 9:30, right on the dot. I rang the bell and waited for him. He took a long time answering, and he was panting slightly when he opened the door. It was easy to guess where he had been, but he had to spell it out for me.

"What a woman!" he oozed. "She goes crazy for me."

I nodded and walked into the house. I sat down in the chair without waiting for an invitation.

"Joe," he said, "I really didn't expect you back so soon. How did it go, boy?"

"Fine," I said. "Smooth as silk, Chief."

"Good," he said. "You've got a head on your shoulders, Joe." He left the room, and came back with another pair of drinks. I took one, only this time I didn't bother to sip it. I threw it right down.

"Now what?" he asked. "Do we just wait till a prowl cop tumbles to it?"

"Relax," I said. "It's all taken care of, Chief."

He gave me a puzzled look, and I stole a glance at my watch. 9:45.

Just then the doorbell rang. He was right on time. The Chief started to stand up, but I beat him to it. "Stay there," I said. "I'll get it." I went to the door and let him in.

He walked in almost apologetically, holding his hat in his hands. "Okay," he said. "I'll deal. Start talking."

The Chief nearly hit the ceiling. "Lucci!" he screamed.

195

ONE NIGHT STANDS

Lucci shrugged. "That's the name," he said. "You wanted to deal, right? Wanted to straighten everything out?"

I couldn't wait much longer. I was afraid the Chief would have an apoplectic fit. I drew the .38 automatic from my pocket and pointed it at the Chief. I fired it three times, and the slugs hit him solidly in the stomach, chest and head. He was dead in almost no time at all.

And just before he died he didn't look powerful at all. He looked weak as a kitten.

I turned to Lucci, and he was utterly dumbfounded. I wiped off the thirty-eight and tossed it on the floor. He looked from the gun to me and back to the gun. The fear danced crazily in his eyes.

"You'd better run," I said. "You'd better run, Lucci."

He ran. I drew slowly, and I fired my .45 just as he reached the door. I shot him three times, too. He died quickly.

Then I sat back and waited. I didn't have long to wait. The prowl cop was right around the corner, and he heard the shots and came running. He took a look at the two men and let out a whoop.

"What happened?"

I pointed to Lucci. "He shot the Chief," I said. "And I shot him."

"Gosh," said the cop. He was a new boy, and this was his first homicide.

"The Chief was cracking down on him," I explained, "and this crumb tried to even things up a little."

"Gosh," repeated the cop. "It's good you shot him. Nice shooting."

"It was an easy shot," I said. "Nothing to it."

"Sure," he said. "But it was a good thing you had your gun."

"We're all required to carry them 24 hours a day."

He shrugged. "Not everyone does, though. It was still good work, Lieutenant."

I smiled at the kid. "Thanks," I said. "But it doesn't bring back the Chief, does it?"

THE WAY TO POWER

I smiled again, sadly. I felt almost like a father to the cop. He was young, but he'd learn.

I wondered if Ruthie was still awake.

I felt powerful as all hell.

YOU CAN'T LOSE

Anyone who starves in this country deserves it. Almost anybody who is dumb enough to want to work can get a job without any backbreaking effort. Blindies and crips haul in twenty-five bucks an hour bumming the Times Square district. And if you're like me—ablebodied and all, but you just don't like to work, all you got to do is use your head a little. It's simple.

Of course, before you all throw up your jobs, let me explain that this routine has its limitations. I don't eat caviar, and East Third Street is a long way from Sutton Place. But I never cared much for caviar, and the pad I have is a comfortable one. It's a tiny room a couple blocks off the Bowery, furnished with a mattress, a refrigerator, a stove, a chair, and a table. The cockroaches get me out of bed, dress me, and walk me down to the bathroom down the hall. Maybe you couldn't live in a place like that, but I sort of like it. There's no problem keeping it up, 'cause it couldn't get any worse.

My meals, like I said, are not caviar. For instance, in the refrigerator right now I have a sack of coffee, a dozen eggs, and part of a fifth of bourbon. Every morning I have two fried eggs and a cup of coffee. Every evening I have three fried eggs and two cups of coffee. I figure, you find something you like, you should stick with it.

And the whole thing is cheap. I pay twenty a month for the room, which is cheap anywhere and amazing in New York. And in this neighborhood food prices are pretty low too.

All in all, I can live on ten bucks a week with no trouble. At the moment I have fifty bucks in my pocket, so I'm set for a month, maybe a little more. I haven't worked in four months, haven't had any income in three.

I live, more or less, by my wits. I hate to work. What the hell,

YOU CAN'T LOSE

what good are brains if you have to work for a living? A cat lives fifty, sixty, maybe seventy years, and that's not a long time. He might as well spend his time doing what he likes. Me, I like to walk around, see people, listen to music, read, drink, smoke, and get a dame. So that's what I do. Since nobody's paying people to walk around or read or anything, I pick up some gold when I can. There's always a way.

By this I don't mean that I'm a mugger or a burglar or anything like that. It might be tough for you to get what I'm saying, so let me explain.

I mentioned that I worked four months ago, but I didn't say that I only held the job for a day. It was at a drugstore on West 96th Street. I got a job there as a stock and delivery boy on a Monday morning. It was easy enough getting the job. I reported for work with a couple of sandwiches in a beat-up gym bag. At four that afternoon I took out a delivery and forgot to come back. I had twenty shiny new Zippo lighters in the gym bag, and they brought anywhere from a buck to a buck-seventy-five at the Third Avenue hock-shops. That was enough money for three weeks, and it took me all of one day to earn it. No chance of him catching me, either. He's got a fake name and a fake address, and he probably didn't notice the lighters were missing for a while.

Dishonest? Obviously, but so what? The guy deserved it. He told me straight off the Puerto Ricans in the neighborhood were not the cleverest mathematicians in the world, and when I made a sale I should short-change them and we'd split fifty-fifty. Why should I play things straight with a bum like that? He can afford the loss. Besides, I worked one day free for him, didn't I?

It's all a question of using your head. If you think things out carefully, decide just what you want, and find a smart way to get it, you come out ahead, time after time. Like the way I got out of going to the army.

The army, as far as I'm concerned, is strictly for the sparrows. I couldn't see it a year ago, and I still can't. When I got my notice I

ONE NIGHT STANDS

had to think fast. I didn't want to try faking the eye chart or anything like that, and I didn't think I would get away with a conscientious objector pitch. Anyway, those guys usually wind up in stir, or working twice as hard as everybody else. When the idea came to me it seemed far too simple, but it worked. I got myself deferred for homosexuality.

It was a panic. After the physical I went in for the psychiatric, and I played the beginning fairly straight, only I acted generally hesitant.

Then the Doc asks, "Do you like girls?"

"Well," I blurt out, "only as friends."

"Have you ever gone with girls?"

"Oh, no!" I managed to sound somewhat appalled at the idea.

I hesitated for a minute or two, then admitted that I was homosexual. I was deferred, of course.

You'd think that everybody who really wanted to avoid the army would try this, but they won't. It's psychological. Men are afraid of being homosexual, or of having people think they're homosexual. They're even afraid of some skull doctor who never saw them before and never will see them again. So many people are so stupid, if you just act a little smart you can't miss. After the examination was over I spent some time with the whore who lives across the hall from me. No sense talking myself into anything. A cat doesn't watch out, he can be too smart, you know.

To get back to my story—the money from the zippos lasted two weeks, and I was practically broke again. This didn't bother me though. I just sat around the pad for a while, reading and smoking, and sure enough, I got another idea that I figured would be worth a few bucks. I showered and shaved, and made a half-hearted attempt at shining my shoes. I had some shoe polish from the drugstore. I had had some room in the gym bag after the zippos, so I stocked up on toothpaste, shoe polish, aspirins, and that kind of junk. Then I put on the suit that I keep clean for emergencies. I usually wear dungarees, but once a month I need a suit for something, so I always

YOU CAN'T LOSE

have it clean and ready. Then, with a tie on and my hair combed for a change, I looked almost human. I left the room, splurged fifteen cents for a bus ride, and got off at Third Avenue and Sixtieth Street. At the corner of Third and 59th is a small semi-hockshop that I cased a few days before. They do more buying-and-selling than actual pawning, and there aren't too many competitors right in the neighborhood. Their stock is average—the more common and lower-priced musical instruments, radios, cameras, record players, and the cheap stuff—clocks, lighters, rings, watches, and so on. I got myself looking as stupid as possible and walked in.

There must be thousands of hockshops in New York, but there are only two types of clerks. The first is usually short, bald, and over forty. He wears suspenders, talks straight to the customers and kowtows to the others. Most of the guys farther downtown fit into this category. The other type is like the guy I drew: tall, thick black hair, light-colored suit, and a wide smile. He talks gentleman-to-gentleman with his upper-class customers and patronizingly to the bums. Of the two he's usually more dangerous.

My man came on with the Johnny-on-the-spot pitch, ready and willing to serve. I hated him immediately.

"I'm looking for a guitar," I said, "preferably a good one. Do you have anything in stock at the moment?" I saw six or seven on the wall, but when you play it dumb, you play it dumb.

"Yes," he said. "Do you play guitar?" I didn't, and told him so. No point in lying all the time. But, I added, I was going to learn.

He picked one off the wall and started plucking the strings. "This is an excellent one, and I can let you have it for only thirty-five dollars. Would you like to pay cash or take it on the installment plan?"

I must have been a good actor, because he was certainly playing me for a mark. The guitar was a Pelton, and it was in good shape, but it never cost more than forty bucks new, and he had a nerve asking more than twenty-five. Any minute now he might tell me that the last owner was an old lady who only played hymns on it I held back the

ONE NIGHT STANDS

laugh and plunked the guitar like a nice little customer.

"I like the sound. And the price sounds about right to me."

"You'll never find a better bargain." Now this was laying it on with a trowel.

"Yes, I'll take it." He deserved it now. "I was just passing by, and I don't have much money with me. Could I make a down payment and pay the rest weekly?"

He probably would have skipped the down payment. "Surely," he said. For some reason I've always disliked guys who say "Surely." No reason, really. "How much would you like to pay now?"

I told him I was really short at the moment, but could pay ten dollars a week. Could I just put a dollar down? He said I could, but in that case the price would have to be forty dollars, which is called putting the gouge on.

I hesitated a moment for luck, then agreed. When he asked for identification I pulled out my pride and joy.

In a wallet that I also copped from that drugstore I have the best identification in the world, all phony and all legal. Everything in it swears up and down that my name is Leonard Blake and I live on Riverside Drive. I have a baptismal certificate that I purchased from a sharp little entrepreneur at our high school back in the days when I needed proof of age to buy a drink. I have a Social Security card that can't be used for identification purposes but always is, and an unapproved application for a driver's license. To get one of these you just go to the Bureau of Motor Vehicles and fill it out. It isn't stamped, but no pawnbroker ever noticed that. Then there are membership cards in everything from the Captain Marvel Club to the NAACP. Of course he took my buck and I signed some papers.

I made it next to Louie's shop at 35th and Third. Louie and I know each other, so there's no haggling. He gave me fifteen for the guitar, and I let him know it wouldn't be hot for at least ten days. That's the way I like to do business.

Fifteen bucks was a week and a half, and you see how easy it was.

YOU CAN'T LOSE

And it's fun to shaft a guy who deserves it, like that sharp clerk did, But when I got back to the pad and read some old magazines, I got another idea before I even had a chance to start spending the fifteen.

I was reading one of those magazines that are filled with really exciting information, like how to build a model of the Great Wall of China around your house, and I was wondering what kind of damn fool would want to build a wall around his house, much less a Great Wall of China type wall, when the idea hit me. Wouldn't a hell of a lot of the same type of people like a Sheffield steel dagger, 25 inches long, an authentic copy of a twelfth century relic recently discovered in a Bergdorf castle? And all this for only two bucks postpaid, no COD'S? I figured they might.

This was a big idea, and I had to plan it just right. A classified in that type of magazine cost two dollars, a post office box cost about five for three months. I was in a hurry, so I forgot about lunch, and rushed across town to the Chelsea Station on Christopher Street, and Lennie Blake got himself a Post Office Box. Then I fixed up the ad a little, changing "25 inches" to "over two feet." And customers would please allow three weeks for delivery. I sent ads and money to three magazines, and took a deep breath. I was now president of Comet Enterprises. Or Lennie Blake was. Who the hell cared?

For the next month and a half I stalled on the rent and ate as little as possible. The magazines hit the stands after two weeks, and I gave people time to send in. Then I went west again and picked up my mail.

A hell of a lot of people wanted swords. There were about two hundred envelopes, and after I finished throwing out the checks and requests for information, I wound up with $196 and sixty-seven 3¢ stamps. Anybody want to buy a stamp?

See what I mean? The whole bit couldn't have been simpler. There's no way in the world they can trace me, and nobody in the Post Office could possibly remember me. That's the beauty of New York—so many people. And how much time do you think the cops will waste looking for a two-bit swindler? I could even have made

203

ONE NIGHT STANDS

another pick-up at the Post Office, but greedy guys just don't last long in this game. And a federal rap I need like a broken ankle.

Right now I'm 100 % in the clear. I haven't heard a rumble on the play yet, and already Lennie Blake is dead-burned to ashes and flushed down the toilet. Right now I'm busy establishing Warren Shaw. I sign the name, over and over, so that I'll never make a mistake and sign the wrong name sometime. One mistake is above par for the course.

Maybe you're like me. I don't mean with the same fingerprints and all, but the same general attitudes. Do you fit the following general description: smart, coldly logical, content with coffee and eggs in a cold-water walk-up, and ready to work like hell for an easy couple of bucks? If that's you, you're hired. Come right in and get to work. You can even have my room. I'm moving out tomorrow.

It's been kicks, but too much of the same general pattern and the law of averages gets you. I've been going a long time, and one pinch would end everything. Besides, I figure it's time I took a step or two up the social ladder.

I had a caller yesterday, a guy named Al. He's an older guy, and hangs with a mob uptown on the West Side. He always has a cigar jammed into the corner of his mouth and he looks like a holdover from the twenties, but Al is a very sharp guy. We gassed around for awhile, and then he looked me in the eyes and chewed on his cigar. "You know," he said, "we might be able to use you."

"I always work alone, Al."

"You'd be working alone. Two hundred a night."

I whistled. This was sounding good. "What's the pitch?"

He gave me the look again and chewed his cigar some more. "Kid," he said, "did you ever kill a man?"

Two hundred bucks for one night's work! What a perfect racket! Wish me luck, will you? I start tonight.

SOURCES

"The Bad Night," *Guilty*, November 1958.
"The Badger Game," *Trapped*, February 1960.
"Bargain in Blood" as by "Sheldon Lord," *Off Beat*, February 1959.
"Bride of Violence," *Two-Fisted*, December 1959.
"The Burning Fury," *Off Beat*, February 1959.
"The Dope," *Guilty*, July 1958.
"A Fire at Night," *Manhunt*, June 1958.
"Frozen Stiff," *Manhunt*, June 1962.
"Hate Goes Courting," *Web*, June 1958.
"I Don't Fool Around," *Trapped*, February 1961.
"Just Window Shopping" as by "Sheldon Lord," *Man's Magazine*, December 1962.*
"Lie Back and Enjoy It," *Trapped*, October 1958.
"Look Death in the Eye," *Web*, April 1959.
"Man with a Passion," *Sure Fire*, July 1958.
"Murder Is My Business," *Off Beat*, September 1958.
"One Night of Death" as by "B. L. Lawrence," *Guilty*, November 1958.
"Package Deal," *Ed McBain's Mystery Book*, # 3, 1961.
"Professional Killer," *Trapped*, April 1959.
"Pseudo Identity," *Alfred Hitchcock's Mystery Magazine*, November 1966.
"Ride a White Horse," *Manhunt*, December 1958.
"A Shroud for the Damned," *Keyhole*, April 1962.
"Sweet Little Racket" as by "B. L. Lawrence," *Trapped*, April 1959.
"The Way to Power," *Trapped*, June 1958.
"You Can't Lose," *Manhunt*, February 1958.

---

* This story was discovered by Lynn Munroe in *Guy*, October 1968; somewhat later Mr. Munroe located an earlier appearance in *Man's Magazine*, December 1962. Lawrence Block recalls that he wrote it for Pontiac Publications around 1957-1958, but its appearance in one of their magazines has not been located.

ONE NIGHT STANDS

One Night Stands by Lawrence Block is printed on 60-pound Glatfelter Supple Opaque recycled acid-free paper, from Times Roman for the text and Albertus Extra Bold for the chapter and running titles. The dust jacket painting and design are by Deborah Miller. The first edition comprises four hundred fifty copies sewn in cloth, signed and numbered by the author, as well as a few out-of-series copies. Each copy includes a separate pamphlet, *Make a Prison*, by Lawrence Block. *One Night Stands* was printed and bound by Thomson-Shore, Inc., Dexter, Michigan, and published in March 1999 by Crippen & Landru Publishers, Norfolk, Virginia.